# ONE TO KEEP

*By Tia Louise*

Jennifer
you're a
Keeper
xoxo

*One to Keep*
Copyright © Tia Louise, 2014
www.facebook.com/AuthorTiaLouise
Printed in the United States of America.

Cover design by Regina Wamba of
**MaeIDesign.com**

*For Mr. TL, to whom I'm tied.*

*No bubblegum required.*

*And to Paul Walker, the original (visual) inspiration for Patrick.*
*Gone too soon.*

# Contents

# CHAPTER 1:

## MORE THAN A SLIP

Either I was being hazed or this was a test.

It was my first day in the Alexander-Knight, LLC, office, sitting in a square-shaped, black leather chair across the desk from my prospective business partner, Derek Alexander, and he wasn't speaking. He was quietly reading my résumé like he should've done before I got here.

To say it was pissing me off would be an understatement.

I could fill in the blanks for him: Patrick Knight, single, retired Guard-turned private investigator.

I was a closer. A deal maker. I looked clients in the eye and told them I'd get their shit done. And I did.

I'd relocated from Chicago to Princeton a month ago to take my older brother Stuart's place at their private investigative firm. A retired Marine, Stuart had taken a job in Saudi Arabia, and his partner Derek needed a replacement. Enter me.

But I wasn't coming here to be treated like a subordinate, and I sure as hell wasn't coming here as Stuart's little brother. So whatever the fuck was going on right now had about five more seconds...

"Sorry." Derek lowered the pages and moved forward in his chair. "I would've read this before you got here, but I just got off a plane." He glanced past his open office door to the blonde sitting out front. "It was supposed to be in my files."

I'd noticed the receptionist when I walked in the door. Bedroom eyes, slim hips, a perfect set of tits—it appeared Alexander-Knight hired the staff for more than their clerical skills. I could work with that. Apology accepted.

"Nice help," I said with a smile.

He blew air through his lips and looked back at my portfolio. "Incompetent."

"But good *under* the desk." It was an attempt at humor, but he didn't take it.

His jaw flexed, and he studied me. "What are your strengths?"

"What?"

"Strengths." His tone was sharp. "What are you good at?"

"You're looking at the list."

"Off the list. What do you prefer?"

My eyebrow rose as I thought about it. I wasn't expecting this question. "Domestic is a pain in the ass. As is kidnapping. I'm not interested in watching the should-be faithful break their vows, and I don't deal with fucked up spouses stealing kids. I won't take crying babies from their mothers."

He nodded. "I understand that."

"Embezzlement, corporate fraud, insider trading... that's the good stuff." I glanced toward the door. "Usually includes a hot secretary ready to spill. With the right motivation."

His brow lowered. "We don't sleep with clients."

I shrugged. "It's not usually necessary—"

"It's never necessary."

Okay, for the record, I got the "don't shit where you eat" rule. But in our business, clients came and went. An occasional dip in the ink was as much a part of the shtick as smoking cigarettes or wearing trench coats. Both of which I guess had gone out of fashion...

"Whatever," I said.

The truth was, I'd never actually slept with a client. I'd always been with Stacy, my ex-fiancée. But the way that had ended revised *all* my former habits. I'd wasted a lot of time being the nice guy, the rule-follower, and I'd had my heart punted like a damn football for it.

It was okay—it was the best thing that could've happened to me, because it brought me to my new understanding: You only live once.

Life was about being lucky and smart, and Derek Alexander was my business partner, not my boss. We did not have to have the same ideas about handling cases. Or clients.

He stood and went to the door. "I'll show you Stuart's old office."

I followed him out, across the open floor-plan. My eyes drifted around the space—dark wood furnishings paired with frosted, etched-glass dividers sporting the A&K logo; clean lines, straight edges. Very professional.

Mine would be the other corner office with a wall of windows overlooking... congested Route 1. "Great view."

He barely noticed. "Stuart said you're good. I'm glad to have you join me if you'd like the job."

What would be my desk was empty except for a slim Macbook. Several bankers' boxes were stacked in the corner.

"Work's been piling up since he left for Saudi."

"I can start today." I held out my hand, and he gave it a brief, firm shake.

"Good. Make yourself at home." Pausing at the door, he looked back. "I'll have Nikki set up your computer and bring you the passwords. She can do that at least."

The last bit was added under his breath, and I assumed Nikki was the pinup out front. I imagined she could do a lot more than setup my computer.

"Thanks," I said.

"Oh, and Patrick, we don't take domestic cases." A hint of a grin—a crack in the wall—was at the corner of his mouth. It was possible this guy might not be such a bad business partner. Stuart wouldn't have sent me here otherwise.

I exhaled a laugh and nodded. "Good."

Turning back to the windows, I stared at the cars clogging up the highway while I waited for Nikki. Princeton wasn't the most exciting place on Earth, but I'd made my choice—this over Afghanistan.

Retired military like Stuart (and me) could get cushy jobs in Middle East security that only lasted three months and paid a shit load of money. But I didn't want to go back there again and again. I was sick of the desert. Instead, I'd come here.

Last week I'd found my apartment and moved all my stuff in, the plasma TV was in place, Bose surround-sound set up—the necessities. After that, I'd spent a few days following up with clients about my move and getting to know the area. Now I was jonesing for a date.

"Good morning, Mr. Knight." Nikki's voice was breathy and high, just like it needed to be. She had those fake, glossy nails that were supposed to look natural, I guessed, and she sat in my chair as she opened the laptop on my desk. Her hand quickly moved the wireless mouse, and her nails clicked against the keys. "I'll just enter all the information, but I'll leave the card with you in case you need it again."

"Thanks." I walked back to where she sat.

Stuart worked in this office six years and never said a word about the eye candy. All he said was Derek needed a partner, and he was trustworthy. I supposed he was also cheap and didn't want to have to change the letterhead and logo—much less the glass doors at the entrance with *Alexander & Knight* lasered into them.

"You can call me Patrick."

Nikki's blue eyes flickered to me briefly from under thick, black lashes then back to the computer. Her lashes were as fake as her too-long, white-blonde hair that was teased up into a side ponytail. But I wasn't judging. The green wrap-dress she wore was skin-tight and stopped at the middle of her smooth, tanned thighs. The girl was stacked, and she clearly took care of herself. I stood behind her shoulder, where I had full view of the dark crack between her nice, round breasts.

"You worked here long?" I hoped she'd lean back a little. She did and lifted her chin, too. Bonus.

11

"A couple months," she said in that voice.

"Like it here?"

"It has its moments." Her tongue touched her bottom lip as she smiled, and her eyes moved from my face, down my chest to my waist, and then slowly up again.

Her full lips were light pink with a darker line around the edges, and I imagined them curving into the shape of an *O*. Her head was just a dip away from my crotch, and my pants grew tight across the fly at the thought of that warm mouth covering me... I was pretty sure we were both thinking the same thing when Derek's voice broke through the tension.

"Nikki, I need to see you in my office."

She blinked and stood, shaking her head as she exhaled, "What now," but she paused at the door. The shiny gold heels she wore flexed her toned calves, and her toenails were painted the same color as her lips. "You're online now. Let me know if you need anything else."

I liked how she said *anything*. I looked forward to working late, needing her assistance, peeling that dress away... Today, however, I was only staying a few hours. I had to finish unpacking my apartment—more specifically, get the bedroom set up—if I planned on having overnight guests.

\* \* \*

The next morning, I carried one box of supplies into my new office. It was early, and Nikki was the only one there, which suited me fine. I wanted to get to know her better.

I left the box on my desk and my blazer on the back of my chair, before going out front again. She was typing up something I couldn't see, and she was as turned out today as she had been yesterday. Today the wrap-dress was pink, and it hugged that amazing rack perfectly. Large gold hoops dangled from her ears, and her thin brows were pulled together over baby blues.

"Mr. Alexander likes to use police codes when he enters the cases into the system," she said as she typed. "But he never worked as a cop."

"I've never worked as a cop either."

I gave her The Smile I used to send panties flying. Her face softened with a laugh, and she held my glance a moment before returning to the computer screen.

"So you're saying I'll have to correct your entries, too?"

"Sounds like you think you know more than me."

When her eyes met mine again, they held a superior look that turned me on even more. "Maybe I do."

I was ready to test that theory in every way. Last night, I'd finished the lair, complete with 800 thread-count sheets and a brand new box of Ultra Thins. "How did you get this knowledge, Ms. Harland?"

"I worked as a dispatcher after high school and all through community college."

That was when I caught the accent. "And where exactly did you do this dispatching?"

"Don't pull that private dick routine on me, Mr. Knight." Her brow arched. "I'm from Corbin, Kentucky."

God, I loved cocky southern women. I could tell she'd be a lot of fun in the sack, and an image of me bending her over that desk, fondling those perfect tits and pounding her as she moaned for more flickered

13

across my mind, causing a stir below my waist. "You might enjoy a little private dick routine from me."

She laughed, not backing down. "What makes you think I don't already have a private dick of my own?"

I was ready to find out when Derek pushed through the glass front doors, ending our banter. Again, he wore a dark suit and tie, and he only briefly assessed my casual appearance. He didn't fool me. The collar-length hair and close beard said a military dress code wasn't his deal. His Gucci look was clearly a personal quirk—one I had no intention of acquiring.

"Good morning, Mr. Alexander," Nikki said, turning back to her computer. She was all business again, but Derek didn't even respond.

He continued past us, only pausing briefly to speak to me. "Would you be able to start on the Alliance Bank case today?"

I gave Nikki a smile and a wink before following the big guy back to his office. "The hacker job?"

"They need a report by Friday if possible. Williams wants to go after the whole ring."

I'd looked at it yesterday afternoon before I left. It was in the top banker's box. A ring of five hackers were pulling the half-cent-add to every transaction con. It didn't sound like much, but with the big banks, it added up fast. And took a while to detect.

"It seems pretty open and shut to me," I said. "Friday shouldn't be a problem."

Derek placed the slim case he carried on his large, mahogany desk and nodded. "Good." He opened his computer and made a few clicks. I started to go, but he stopped me. "Any interest in going to Scottsdale in a few weeks?"

"Arizona?" I frowned. "At the hottest time of the year? Why?"

"I've been invited to do a security workshop for a banker's conference, but I'd rather stick close and keep an eye on Wallace Trading." He sat and leaned back in his leather chair. "I was planning to turn it down, but you could take it. It's a good way to meet new clients."

"How soon do you need to know?"

He stood and moved a few files around like he was searching for something. "A-sap."

I nodded, starting for the door. "I'll think about it."

* * *

The box holding my work essentials was in the center of my desk, and for a moment, I surveyed the contents—an old Bears mug, a couple of hardbound legal texts I used pretty regularly, a baseball-shaped stress ball, a now-empty picture frame.

I pulled the ball out and gave it a squeeze while I considered moving the entire contents to the dumpster—saving the books, of course. All the other shit brought my former life back too irritatingly close for comfort.

Still holding the ball, I leaned back in my chair with one of the books. Nikki's comment about correcting my reports was in my head, and I was pretty sure this one had police codes in the index. Feet on the desk, I saw what I thought was a piece of cardboard stuck between the pages, but when I flipped it over, it was more like a million iron-fisted slams straight to the gut. Stacy.

My kid sister Amy had taken this picture of us at the Navy Pier a year ago—the day I'd proposed. The day she'd said yes, knowing she was screwing my neighbor.

My jaw clenched as I studied my blissed-out expression. What a joke.

Her blonde hair ended in the slightest flip at her shoulders, and I looked like a first-class sucker with my arms around her waist, kissing her cheek. I was only twenty-seven when we met, and two years later I proposed. In hindsight, I decided my feelings were a combination of feeling like it was "time," whatever the fuck that means, and of her being the first woman I'd connected with after Afghanistan.

Either way, she did not share my level of commitment.

It was a really classy send-off, too. Her in my kitchen, on her back on my bar, moaning with her knees spread wide. The dick from 24B had his face buried between her thighs, and he was going to town.

Fuck the tightness in my chest. I crushed the glossy print in my fist and leaned back, slamming the stress ball hard as I could against the opposite wall.

*CRASH!* My aim was too high, and the large, black-and-white framed art photo was now shattered. Shit.

"Oh my god, what happened?" Nikki was breathless as she rushed into my office, but I was already across the room, taking down the frame. Glass was everywhere.

"My hand slipped." I didn't turn around. I was pretty sure remnants of anger were still on my face, but I kept my back to her, trying to hide it.

"Sounds like a lot more than a slip." Her tone said she was onto me as she took the picture. "Poor Wilson."

"Wilson?"

"The tiger whose picture you smashed. It's from the university." She only paused a moment before going to the door. "Hang on, we keep a vacuum in the kitchen closet. Don't cut yourself."

I bent down and started collecting the larger fragments and tossing them in the trash. *Bee stings... needles... rope burns... glass cuts.* It was a game Stuart and I made up when we were kids. Who could name the worst kind of pain. Those were real injuries, that Stacy flashback was bullshit.

"Here, stand back." Nikki positioned the long silver hose and bent over to capture the splinters of glass.

I leaned forward to retrieve the stress ball, and shiny heels lifted her ass almost directly in my face. Wrapped in that tight pink dress that hit mid-thigh, the view reminded me the best way to kill bad memories. I was inches from sliding my fingers between her legs, teasing her soft folds, dipping a finger inside — I could almost hear her satisfied sighs. Sure I played the field, but at least I was a gentleman about it. Ladies always came first.

Watching her derriere sway a bit longer, I wondered how I could get a read on her feelings about the matter. I was pretty sure she was considering it this morning. Just then, I noticed Derek standing in the doorway watching us.

"What happened?" His voice sounded more annoyed than concerned.

"Stress balls don't bounce." I tossed it up and caught it as I stood. My fantasy of fingering Nikki had me feeling better as I went back to my desk.

She switched off the vacuum. "That should be all of it," she said, carrying the appliance to the door.

"How much longer on those emails?" Derek asked as she passed.

"I'll have them to you by lunch." I could see she was irritated by his question, but I was pretty sure he couldn't. "I can't predict when one of you's going to tear your office apart."

"Oh, sorry, Nik," I called after her. "And thanks."

She didn't answer, but Derek cut in, still seeming annoyed. "You doing anything after work today?"

As a matter of fact, I hoped to be doing something soft and pink, and she was headed back to her workstation right at that moment.

"Why?" I was already plotting my approach.

"Building E has a fitness center. It's part of the complex, so we get a free membership with rent."

My eyes went to my senior partner's. "Good to know."

"I need a spotter, and you look like you could work off some steam."

Sitting in my chair, I had to laugh. "Look, Derek. You're a hot piece of ass—I'm secure enough to say it—but I'm straight."

That dark brow lowered over his blue eyes, and I could tell he could probably be one scary motherfucker when he needed to be. "Fuck you, too," he said. "Be at the gym at five. On time."

Exhaling loudly, I leaned back in my chair, squeezing the stress ball. He was probably right. Screwing Nikki could ultimately backfire. Still, I'd be damned if I went much longer without getting laid.

## Chapter 2:
## Removal of Long-Story Stacy

Derek loaded the bar to 285 and stood at my head as I lay back on the bench. "See how many you can do."

I'd started exercising pretty regularly after my breakup. It filled the time and deadened the pain. It also had perks, as most women (all women?) appreciated a cut naked torso as opposed to a flabby one. Still, I wasn't near as jacked as my partner here.

He'd overloaded the bar for me, and I was pretty sure he knew it. But hell if I was backing down from this pissing contest. I gripped the metal, inhaled deeply, and pressed. Immediately, the burn shot down the backs of my arms. I lowered it, tightened my abs, and pushed up again. Derek caught it at the top and guided it back to the rack.

"Good," he said, walking around to take my spot as I sat up.

I took his place, pressing my lips together as I helped him guide the bar off the rack again. He did a set of four before returning it. *Dick.*

While he recovered, I adjusted the strap on my glove. "How long you been working out?"

"Going on five years." He pushed his dark hair out of his face. That with the beard made him look like a beefed-up, blue-eyed Jesus.

"*After* the Marines?"

"After my wife died." He said it in a way that didn't invite questions. I didn't ask, but hell if I wasn't curious.

"I started about a year ago." Then I turned on The Smile. "It helps to look good for the ladies."

"Does that include Stacy?"

I had enough self-control not to pop him one. "Stuart tell you about that?"

"Just reading your arm. Didn't mean to touch a nerve." He stood and walked over to grab his water bottle.

Fucking tattoo. I looked down at my inner forearm where I'd had her name inked in a cursive script. "Know anybody who can help me with this?"

For the first time he laughed. "As a matter of fact, I do." Pulling up his sleeve, I saw the requisite *SF*-with-eagle tattoo all Marines had somewhere on their bodies.

"That's good work," I said.

"I've known Carl a while. Runs a clean shop, and I handled a case for him last year. He's a good guy."

"I thought you didn't take domestic cases."

"I make exceptions for old friends. Sometimes."

We started curl reps using oversized dumbbells. Derek's were about a third larger than mine, but I wasn't competing with him. I already had an older brother to bust my balls.

"What's the name?" I hissed through an exhale.

"Living Arts. It's not too far from downtown." He exhaled a lift. "I'll put in a call for you."

"That's okay," I said dropping the weights. All the Stacy talk had me done for the day. "I can take care of myself. See you tomorrow."

"Thanks for helping me out."

I paused and looked back for a second. Then I remembered his comment about his late wife, and decided not to be a shit. "I guess I could do this more. How often you come up here?"

He set the dumbbells down and picked up his towel and water bottle. "Couple times a week."

"Let me know next time, and I'll join you."

He agreed as I picked up my phone and headed out to the parking lot.

* * *

Nikki greeted me perky as always the next morning. Today she wore denim capris and a blue top that reminded me of something a pirate might own. The open collar slung low around her neck and off one shoulder, revealing her soft cleavage.

Working out took the edge off last night, but I'd woken up with a raging hard-on this morning. Beating off in the shower sucked, and my arms were sore from lifting more than I was used to. I was ready to relax into the real thing—soft, warm, and wet.

"Are you turning into a muscle head like Derek?" She smiled, and I considered asking her out right then, to hell with office protocol.

Her hair hung loose down her back, and all I could think of was pulling her onto my lap, sliding my hands under that top, my thumbs across her tight nipples. Shit, if I wasn't getting a semi envisioning it.

"I don't want to look juiced," I said. "But I'll probably meet up with him some during the week."

"Stuart never did."

"Right. I guess you knew my brother?"

Her eyes went back to her laptop. "Mm-hm." The way she said it, all wistful like she was remembering something... Had Nikki and Stuart been together? Shit. That threw a wrench in my plans. I wasn't interested in swimming in his wake.

"Yeah, he never worked out." I tried to recover. "Say, Nik," I stayed by her desk. It was just the two of us in the office, and I had another question on my mind. "Derek said something about his wife yesterday."

Her eyes widened. "He did?"

I paused, slightly taken aback. "What happened? Was she killed?"

"Oh, no." She shook her head and leaned back in her chair. "She died about six years ago. Cancer, I think. Stuart said they were childhood sweethearts or something. She waited for him to come back from overseas and they got married."

"Were they married long?"

She shrugged. "I don't know. Derek never talks about it. As in *never*. And as far as I know he never dates anyone."

For a moment I chewed the inside of my cheek, thinking. Being loyal I could understand. Hell, I could still remember the devotion I felt when I'd proposed to Stacy, but six years was a long time to be alone. I wasn't sure how that changed my opinion of my new partner. How much alike that made us.

*Formerly* alike.

The soft noise of a throat clearing brought me back. I blinked to find Nikki narrowing her eyes at me.

"What?" Coming out of my distraction, I realized my eyes had been lingering on her breasts.

"Leave something on me, I might catch a cold."

I coughed a laugh. "Sorry, I didn't mean to —"

"Oh, please. I've watched those sexy hazel eyes undress me for two days." She stood and picked up her smartphone. "There's a coffee shop in Building C. You could at least buy me a drink after all that action."

"Sure," I said, checking the clock. It was 7:45. The office didn't officially open until nine. Forget Stuart. Forget Derek and one-sided loyalties. I was following my new philosophy now, and ready to see how far this might go.

* * *

Nikki sipped the hot beverage, her pink lips lined as always in a darker rose. "No coffee for you?"

"No." We walked slowly back to the Alexander-Knight offices. "I like coffee, but when it's hot like this, not as much."

She nodded. "I'm addicted. I could have coffee all day long in any weather."

In the center of the cluster of five buildings was a round courtyard with benches and a tall, obelisk-shaped fountain. We paused for a moment to watch the water rippling down the sides of the smooth concrete, and I wondered how to get us on the subject of us.

Nikki broke the silence. "So tell me about Patrick Knight," she said, giving me that cocky glance. "Why is a hot young thing like you single and relocating from Chicago to Princeton?"

"Wow," I laughed. "You know a lot already."

"I handle the office paperwork, remember?"

"Right," I nodded as we started walking again. "It's simple. Broke up with my fiancée, wanted to start somewhere fresh."

"So you're a heartbreaker." Nikki winked as she sipped again.

"Nope. I was the one getting his insides kicked out that time." Exhaling, I just said it. "Caught her screwing a guy in my building."

Nikki's thin brows pulled together, and she touched my arm. "I'm so sorry, Patrick."

My hand covered hers briefly. "No worries, it's ancient history. And Stuart said this was a great gig."

She took another sip as she nodded. "Stuart was a lot of fun. You remind me of him."

"He tries to be as cool as me."

She laughed, her thick lashes fluttering as she rolled her eyes. "You're too much."

"How long have you worked here?" I studied her profile, her small, upturned nose and those full lips I wanted to taste, as we pushed through the heavy metal doors of Building A.

"Three months, but it's a pretty straightforward office."

"Except for the hard-ass boss?" I held the door for her.

"Derek's just like every entrepreneur I've ever worked for." She leaned against the marble wall, waiting for the elevator. "He has his own ideas of how to do things, and he isn't a very good communicator." Then she added in a sneaky tone. "He really needs to get laid."

I smiled, but that comment stopped me. "Were you planning to help him with his problem?"

"No." Her lips parted over straight, white teeth. "But I was sorry to see Stuart go."

Her eyes traveled from my face to my lips briefly as the elevator doors opened. The more I thought about it, the more I was sure if my older brother *had* bagged Nikki, I'd have heard about it. Talk about a braggart.

We stepped inside, and when the doors closed, I leaned closer, lowering my voice. "My brother's an idiot if he didn't notice you. Why don't you let me make up for his mistake?"

"You're too young for me, Patrick." Her voice was equally low, and she didn't make eye contact.

I rubbed a hand roughly through the top of my light brown hair. It hadn't been cut since I left Chicago and still have the remnants of summer highlighting in the tips. "I need a trim. This makes me look younger."

Nikki smiled as she studied me. "I like it. It's sexy and summery."

"I look like a frat boy."

She laughed. "You look like my boss. Otherwise, it's a very tempting offer."

Our bodies were still close, and she turned back to the control panel. Heat radiated between us, and if I leaned slightly forward, I could take her lips. Soft at first, then deeper. "What are you? Thirty-two?"

"Rude!"

That made me laugh. "You started it!"

She exhaled, shaking her head and stepping away as the doors opened. "Add five and you win."

I hung back, admiring how those capris hugged her ass. "Seven years is not that much older."

"You're only saying that because you're horny."

"You only live once."

"Exactly." She turned away from me and back to her computer. "Find a girl closer to your own age."

At that I shrugged, "Suit yourself."

Neither waiting nor begging was my style. She might change her mind with a little break to think about it, and in the meantime, I had to take care of my other problem. Opening my laptop, I typed in "Living Arts" and "tattoos." A professional-looking website popped up, and I grabbed my phone, punching in the address.

This afternoon, I'd have the final evidence of my irritating past removed.

\* \* \*

Living Arts Tattoo Parlor was located in what appeared to be the head part of town. It was squeezed between a shop that specialized in likely illegal pot paraphernalia and another that had nothing but crystals of all shapes and sizes hanging in the windows. It was nearly impossible to imagine Mr. Gucci Alexander coming here for anything.

Figuring I'd have to stay a few hours, I'd stopped by my apartment and changed into faded blue jeans and a T-shirt. When I'd had the tattoo put on, a biker chick and two inked-up guys cultivating the ex-con look had run that establishment. Entering Living Arts, I didn't expect to see a petite girl—woman?—waiting behind the counter for the next customer.

Her skin was ivory-white and contrasted starkly with her artificially black hair and red-velvet lips. At first glance her hair appeared long and swept over her shoulder, but the closer I got, I realized it was actually cut short on one side, tapering off at an angle and down the other. Asymmetrical or whatever.

I was ready to dismiss her when she hit me with a pair of ice blue eyes that made my stomach tighten. They were beautiful, although when they met mine they narrowed and blinked down to the counter. Her lips pressed together into a frown.

I didn't know what any of that meant, and I didn't care. *Shit*, Nikki was right. I was too keyed up for my own good. Shaking it off, I glanced around to see who might work on my arm. A beefy skinhead covered in ink was chatting and working on another guy getting what looked like a full-back tat. They'd be a while. Nobody else was in the place, so I turned back to the girl.

"Hey," I said and waited.

Her hands fluttered over a stack of papers on the counter, and she didn't look up. "Can I help you?" Her voice was small but defiant.

She still wouldn't look at me, so I allowed my eyes to travel over her thin body. Dark jeans were slung low on her hips, and they were so tight, they made her look like she had an ass, which I was pretty sure she didn't. Above a thin strip of pale mid-drift she had on a black, transparent blouse that draped over one shoulder. A black tube top was underneath, and her skin was smooth and free of ink. Odd.

"Yeah," I cleared my throat, double-checking for anyone else. "I have a reworking job for... somebody."

That's when her eyes met mine again, but now hers were confused. "Reworking?"

I gave her The Smile, and she blinked quickly away, seeming irritated. Ignoring her response, I stretched my arm out to her, palm up.

"I think there's a rule that as soon as you get their name tattooed on you, it's over."

She studied the cursive *Stacy* on my inner forearm, and for whatever reason, that broke the ice slightly. Her red lips parted over straight white teeth. "What happened with Stacy?"

"Long story," I said. "Can somebody help me?"

She exhaled as she leaned down then hefted a huge binder containing plastic-coated sheets onto the counter. Flipping large chunks over and over, she stopped in the back on a page of line drawings.

"I'd suggest turning it into a barbed wire band or maybe something Aztec." Her slim finger pointed to one design. Short, neat nails painted black, of course. A silver band was on the thumb of her left hand. "This one's pretty common, but I can do some variations to make it unique if you like."

"You been doing this long?" I wasn't sure it was such a great idea to get ink from a tattoo virgin.

She shook her head, keeping her eyes on the drawings. "I was a fine arts major in college. Then after…" Her throat cleared. "I needed a job. Carl showed me how to work the equipment."

I noticed her near-slip, but let it pass. "A fine artist?"

"Yeah."

"So I guess your biggest problem was fear of needles."

"Oh, you don't see the needle." She was starting to relax and make eye contact more. Still there was something up with her, a guard or something. It had me curious. "It's more like illustrating with an ink gun. The blood was the worst part for me."

My arm flinched back at that. "I've never bled getting a tattoo."

"It only happens once in a while." Her silky hair swished over her right shoulder as her head moved. For a split second, I wished it was all there. The way the right side hung in long waves, I could tell she'd be pretty without her disguise on.

"I faint at the sight of blood."

"At least you share the pain." I teased, hoping to diffuse the remaining tension. "But let's try and avoid that drama with me."

"So you want me to do it?" She walked around the counter, and I got the full view — including the shoes. Her skinny jeans ended at black and brown, needle-thin stripper heels.

"Those are some shoes," I said. "How tall are you for real?"

A little color appeared in her cheeks, and it softened her looks so much, I wanted to make it happen again. "Five foot." She pulled out a sketch pad and wrote *Stacy* in almost the exact script of my arm.

"You'd make a good forger."

The pink stayed on her cheeks, and in five more quick strokes, she'd turned it into a design that was completely unrecognizable as a name. Then she turned the pad toward me.

"Damn, girl. You're good."

*Bingo*. Red flooded her face, and she was all softness, defenses down. She looked really pretty. "I've been at it about six months."

"Let's get started."

She nodded and led me back to a chair with a table attached. An assortment of inks was arranged on a rack, and she picked up the gun and a few tips. "I didn't ask if you wanted color."

"Plain black is fine."

She nodded and went to the cabinet, pulling down a narrow-headed, disposable razor, alcohol, and a cotton ball.

Carl's voice snapped from the back where he was working. "Kenny." He didn't sound mean, but definitely stern. "You forgot the paperwork."

She dropped the cotton ball, and her hand pushed the short side of her hair back. "Oh my god, I never forget that." It was said more to herself, so I didn't answer. Truth was, I'd forgotten it, too.

"I'm sorry." She quickly went back to the desk. I couldn't believe how fast she could move and still stay upright in those shoes. In a flash, she was back with a clipboard, pointing to the different paragraphs as she spoke. "It's basically a standard consent form. You verify you're not intoxicated, don't have HIV to your knowledge, the basics."

"No problem." I signed on the dotted line, and she took it back then returned to pick up where she'd left off.

"I'm going to shave your arm here," she said, smoothing two fingers over my forearm. "It won't be as noticeable since your hair's pretty fine anyway." With a gentle, but firm touch, she turned my arm over and ran the razor across my skin.

"How long do you think this will take?"

This girl was not my type at all, but still I hoped she'd say it would take a while. I liked looking at her.

Slim, dark brows pulled together. "An hour? Maybe two?"

"Sounds good."

She returned my smile at last, and I noticed a cute little dimple piercing her left cheek. "I need to make the stencil."

Quickly she took a carbon and removed the brown protective layer, then just as fast, she traced the sketch she'd made on top of the papers. In two moves, she'd pulled it out and applied it to my skin. As she leaned over me, I caught a light scent of sugary perfume, and again my stomach tightened.

"You shouldn't tell anyone you've only been doing this six months," I said.

The dimple was back, and her cool blue eyes met mine as she pulled on black gloves and screwed the ink onto the gun. "Do I look like a professional?"

"Yes."

She took out a sterile pad, cleaned my skin, and got to work. Her gaze was steady, and it only stung a little as she quickly made a stroke, followed by a quick wipe. Stroke, wipe, stroke, wipe. The repetition continued as the braided design took shape and my past disappeared.

"Does it distract you if I talk?" I said, watching her.

She only paused a beat to smile up at me, shake her head, and then blink back down to my arm.

"Were you planning to be a tattoo artist when you finished school?"

Dimple. "No, but I like the work. Carl's a good boss."

"But no ink for you?"

"Oh, I have a tattoo. A couple, actually."

I immediately wanted to see them. "Are they hidden?"

She did a final swipe and put the gun down. "The first one's here." Pulling the latex glove down half-way, she opened her palm, and I saw a small teardrop in the center. My thoughts derailed at the sight of it and what I knew to be the meaning.

Now my brows pulled together as I studied her face. Despite the heavy, cat-eye liner and deep red lips, I didn't see it. She seemed too young and innocent to have a teardrop tattooed in her hand. So I played dumb.

"Does that have a meaning?"

Restoring the glove, she barely nodded and resumed her work. The original guard was back in place, and now her expression contained a new emotion—sadness.

"You said Carl hired you *after.*" My voice was low. "After what?"

Another stroke, another swipe, before she answered. "After college. What else?" This time the smile was fake, no dimple.

I nodded and dropped it. To my knowledge, Derek hadn't called before I came, so she didn't know what I did for a living. "Your name's Kenny?"

Her eyes briefly met mine, then she nodded.

"Is that short for something?"

"Kendra."

"Kendra...?"

"Woods." She paused before turning my arm to finish the other side. "What do you think?"

"I think it looks really good." A slight pink puffiness was around the woven lines, but her work was clean. "And I like that it's original art."

That brought back the dimple. "I'll call it 'Removal of Long-Story Stacy.'"

"Would you go out with me?"

*What the hell?* I'd said it without even thinking. At the same time, it made a lot better sense for me to be with her than with Nikki.

Actually it made no sense, but I'd go with it.

She laughed, high and sweet. "You're asking me out? You?"

I couldn't help being a little offended. "What does that mean?"

"We do not go together." She shook her head. "You're like… Captain America or Mr. Bingley…"

"I prefer the former."

"Good, because I'm no Jane Bennett."

"Could you be Peggy Carter?"

Again her brow creased. "Who's that?"

"Captain America's…" *Shit.* I wasn't about to say girlfriend. I wasn't even sure why I'd asked her out. Fucking curiosity, I guessed. "Nevermind. Let's get a drink."

"You shouldn't drink alcohol for twenty-four hours. You could bleed."

"Tomorrow then. It's Friday. I'll pick you up after work."

The dimple was joined by the pink cheeks, and she looked down. "You can buy me a drink tomorrow after work, but you need to know I'm leaving."

"After one drink?" My thumb was at her forearm, and I lightly slid it along her skin. "Maybe you'll enjoy my company more than you think."

Strangely, my touch didn't seem to bother her as much as the eye contact. "No, Princeton. I'm leaving town, moving back to Bayville next week."

"Okay." That could actually work in my favor, depending on what happened. "We'll make it your last night on the town."

She seemed confused, but she agreed. "Whatever you say." Putting the gun down, she leaned back and stretched. Her skinny torso lengthened, and I couldn't help thinking of a cat. "All done."

Holding my arm up, I twisted it around. "I like it. Thanks." We walked back to the front, and I handed her my card to pay. "So I'll pick you up here tomorrow night at... what?"

"I should be finished here by seven-thirty." She handed my card back with a receipt and the standard after-tat directions and care kit. The look in her eyes was interested but still cautious, which was fine. The feeling was mutual.

I signed the papers and gave her a wink. "See you tomorrow."

## CHAPTER 3:
### DANGEROUSLY SWEET

Kenny was a different person on Friday. Well, she was dressed similarly to the day before in a filmy blue top over a black tank with skinny jeans, but the resistance seemed gone. She teetered out on blue-suede stilettos that let her toenails (also painted black) peep out, and she greeted me with a smile and a kiss on the cheek, sending that sugary perfume all around me. She was like a licorice pixie stick in heels.

"Nice shoes," I said.

She narrowed one eye as she continued past me. "I'll see if they come in your size."

Her smart remark caught me by surprise, but I liked it. Feisty was always a win in my book. It usually translated to hot sex, which was potentially somewhere on the table for tonight.

"I'll take it that's your way of saying *Thank you*." I helped her into my waiting Charger before going to the driver's side. "You're too skinny. I'm buying you a pizza before the night's over."

She shook her head. "Lactose intolerant."

"Then we'll hold the cheese."

We were headed to O'Harry's pub, a microbrewery a few blocks away. I figured it was neutral enough for starters. We'd see where it went from there. She was right about one thing, we were an odd couple.

"Is it possible to get pizza without cheese?"

"I don't know, but we'll find out."

Inside the pub, we were two of a handful of patrons, but it was early. I ordered us each a beer before Kenny cut me off. "I'll have a frozen margarita."

"I don't think—" Her black-tipped finger pointed to a swirling frozen drink machine hidden in the back corner. Shaking my head, I had to laugh.

"There are actually people who don't like beer," she said in that tone. "Can you believe it?"

It was like I was back in college, buying frozen drinks for underage girls. "How old are you anyway?"

"So we've passed the pleasantries and gone straight to rude."

"Hey, you started it."

"I'm twenty-four." Her chin lifted, but I shook my head.

"Baby." I lifted my beer and took a long sip.

"And you're..."

"Older than twenty-four."

Thirty wasn't *that* much older, but my conversation with Nikki had me feeling a little superior. She took a hard pull from her straw, and I couldn't tell if she got any of the frozen drink. I took another easy sip of beer.

"I like this version of you better," I said. "Yesterday you acted like you either wanted to run or punch me in the mouth."

"I did not." That blush was on her cheek again, and I turned on my stool to face her.

"Yes, you did. So why the switch?"

She took another hard pull on the straw, and with a little growl, she pulled the top off the cup, drinking a large mouthful that way. I couldn't help but grin as she repeated the process and then sat straighter, pushing the long side of her hair over her shoulder.

"After you left, Carl told me you work with Derek, which makes you a good guy." She cocked a dark brow at me. "But with that body and those hazel eyes, you're too good-looking. And you know it."

I exhaled a laugh and turned back to the bar, lifting my beer again. When I glanced back, her expression had changed. Now she was studying me like I was the puzzle. "So what's your story? Why are you here with me?"

"I could say the same to you."

She shook her head and took another mouthful of frozen margarita. "Not on your first night."

I nodded. "I agree. Moving along. Explain this Bingley thing."

Her head ducked with her laugh, and that dimple appeared. "Bingley is a character from *Pride and Prejudice*. He's all Mr. Sunny, rich and handsome. The perfect nice guy."

My jaw clenched, but I let her continue.

"Compared to the dark and brooding Mr. Darcy."

"I take it you've met Derek."

"Only once." She poked the frozen drink with her straw. "He has a really good reputation."

I waved over the bartender, who pointed at my drink. "Another beer?"

"No—vodka. Neat."

Kenny's eyebrows rose.

"I'm in the mood for something stronger."

"Make that two," she said before our server left.

"You're mixing?"

"I'm in the mood for something stronger, too."

Two vodkas later, we were filling in all the blanks.

"God, I fucking don't want to go home," she said, resting her forehead on her hand.

My brow creased. "Then why do it?"

She exhaled and churned her straw in and out of the margarita that now only had two frozen chunks left. "It'll be better." She didn't look up. "Once I face all the jerks who told me not to leave with him in the first place."

I lifted the beer I still had and took a sip. "It won't be so bad. Everybody has to leave home. So what if you're going back?"

"It's the *way* I left." She shook her lop-sided hair. "Everybody hated me with Blake. My mom called crying every day after we moved here."

I set the mug down and slid my finger along the frosted side of the glass. "What was he, an ex-con?"

"Only if juvie counts."

"Okay," I turned in my seat and caught her left hand, opening her palm to expose the teardrop. "What's this about?"

She shrugged. "I wanted to remember him somehow. I cried for so long after he died, I put a tear in my hand."

"But you know that's prison code for murder."

"Yes, Carl already told me. I'm a dumbass." She pulled her hand back and examined the little black drop. Her voice grew quieter. "But it makes sense to me."

"He was killed in a barfight?" I'd done a little snooping back at the office.

She nodded, still looking at her hand. "Professional fighter beat him to death. Derek helped put the guy away."

We were quiet then. I wasn't sure what to say to her, if she needed comforting or if that would make her feel awkward. She put on a tough show, but I wasn't buying it. Her easy blush for one gave away how young she still was.

The sounds of the bar were louder now that the after-work crowd was growing. More groups of guys were forming half-circles, laughing and shouting, while televisions blasted a soccer game from somewhere else in the world.

Kenny suddenly dropped her hand and looked up at me. "Let's go dancing!"

"What?" I shook my head, sitting up straighter. "I'm no dancer."

"Come on." She hopped off her stool and grabbed my arm. "There's a club across the parking lots. It's pretty much a wannabe rave, but it's better than this sausage fest."

With an exhale, I stood and fished out enough cash to cover our tab. Her story had mellowed my fight, and I didn't feel like just sitting and drinking anymore. "You really want to dance?"

"Yes," she took a long sip, squinting as she polished off the margarita. "I'm tired of being sad."

\* \* \*

In less than five minutes we were in the dark club. Electronic music blasted, and black lights illuminated plastic glow-stick accessories and anything white. Kenny went straight to the floor, rotating her hips and moving her arms in time to the music. I went to the bar and ordered another beer. For a while I watched her. Her eyes were closed, and her tiny body twisted gracefully in those crazy shoes. She seemed lost in the repetitive song. Then it morphed into something new, and her eyes opened to meet mine.

She walked to where I leaned against the bar and took my hands, placing them on her hips. "Why aren't you dancing?"

Her hands went to my shoulders, and she swayed in front of me. In the flashing lights of the bar, all I could see were her blue eyes. She smiled and that dimple appeared.

"Your story beats mine by a longshot," I said, unsure how I wanted to feel about her. The whole fact of us here, together, touching each other this way seemed out of left field. But at the same time, it wasn't a bad thing out of left field.

Her eyes closed as she leaned into my ear. "What's your story, Bingley?"

I shrugged. "Cheating fiancée. Fucking a guy in my building, and I caught them."

Her voice was still at my ear. "Bitch."

"Yeah," I said, the alcohol making me talk. "She wanted something different, said I was too safe... whatever the fuck that means."

Pressing my shoulders, Kenny leaned back, and her blue eyes held mine. "You're not safe. You're dangerously sweet."

"That doesn't make any sense."

She smiled and ran a finger across my chest. "I bet you get any girl you want."

My efforts to get Nikki crossed my mind. "Not always."

"Buy me another drink."

"I think you've had enough."

"Fuck that." Her hand returned to my shoulder. "Let's both be dangerous."

My lips pressed into a frown, but I waved the bartender over and ordered a vodka for me, another margarita for her. She sipped from the salty glass, watching me with those round eyes, but I looked away. She was leaving in a week.

\* \* \*

Another hour, another vodka, and I was dancing. We were both on the floor, and Kenny went from twisting in front of me with her arms around my neck to turned away from me, her skinny ass scrubbing against my dick. It was just fucking dancing. I wasn't trying to get turned on, but I was never sure how that dance was supposed to be interpreted.

For the first time in a while, my insides didn't ache, that residual sting had disappeared. It was like the last reminders of Stacy were gone, but I knew it was just the alcohol. I'd been here before, and the pain always came back. When the song ended, I was ready to call it a night.

I caught Kenny's waist and pulled her to me, speaking in her ear. "It's late—let's take off."

She nodded and followed me back to the bar, took a finishing drink as I paid, and then we left.

Crossing the parking lots back to where I'd left the car, I couldn't tell which of us was working harder to walk a straight line. I won, but only because I wasn't balancing on those heels. When we reached my Charger, I leaned heavily against the door.

"I can't drive like this." I said through an exhale, scanning the parking lot. We were the only ones out here, and it was dark. I didn't like it. "Get in."

She wobbled around the car, and I managed to guide her into the passenger's side. Then I went around and climbed in, locking the doors. Kenny was busy removing her shoes, and I pressed my head against the headrest.

"It's okay," she said, sitting up and putting her hand on my shoulder. "We can just make out til we sober up."

"Make out?" My brow creased. "What happened to 'don't get any ideas' and you leaving?"

She shook her head and scooted toward me. "This is not about ideas. This is just about sobering up."

The alcohol, I'm sure, made her logic seem reasonable. That, and her grinding against my dick was still pretty fresh in my inebriated mind. She put her cool hands on my cheeks and then slid them back into my hair. I leaned forward and lightly brushed my lips over hers. They were soft and warm, and a little salty from the margaritas. She smiled and pressed her mouth harder against mine, sneaking her tongue out and touching my lips before she leaned back. Fuck, that felt good.

I caught her face and kissed her for real then, pulling her full bottom lip gently between my teeth as I finished. A little noise escaped her throat, and it was like a match being struck. Our kisses turned fast and desperate, mouths opened, tongues collided. Her slim arms pulled her body against mine, and I lifted her easily into the backseat, not caring if we were still in the parking lot. We were in a dark space in the back, and I wasn't stopping this.

I bruised her small mouth with kisses as she struggled to move higher on the seat to meet me. I should've been gentler, but dammit I couldn't. The tiny moans coming from her throat told me she didn't mind my roughness. She was as feverish as I was.

Moving my hands down, I caught the hem of her blouse and shoved everything up — shirt, under-tank, and bra. Her small breasts popped out, and I pulled a tight, pink bud into my mouth, sucking it hard.

"Oh, god," she moaned, her fingers going into my hair, holding my head against her body. I kissed a line across the center to the other side, finding her other nipple, and sliding my tongue around it. That faint scent of sugar was on her skin, and she even tasted sweet. I moved up to cover her mouth again and noticed she was pulling on the back of my shirt. I took a second to lean back and whip it over my head.

"Jesus," she hissed, reaching out to run her fingers down my stomach.

"What?" My voice was a hoarse whisper as I took a quick hit off her mouth again.

She turned her face, and I nipped her earlobe. "Your body... Oh, god."

Her voice went breathless again as my hands worked to slide her tight jeans down her narrow hips. Working my way down to her belly, I kissed her flat, white stomach before reaching the top of her panties.

Any rational thought was gone. I'd been without this too long, and I didn't care what happened when we finished. Her body was squirming, following my mouth, and I saw a small patch of dampness on the front of her blue thong.

"Fuck me," I muttered, pulling it aside and sinking my tongue into her bare folds.

"Ohh!" She wailed as my tongue tasted her soft, warm clit. "Oh, god yes." Her hips were bucking, and my cock was straining against my zipper. She was seriously getting off, and I was ready to plunge inside. Instead, I slid two fingers in, making sure. She was dripping, her inner muscles flexing as my fingers moved in and out of her.

"Oh, Patrick!" She wailed, grinding her hips as her hands went over her head to the car door and then just as fast back to my head. "Oh, god, don't stop!"

I had no intention of stopping. I kissed and sucked her clit as she moaned and twisted against my mouth. My fingers worked her, in and out a few more times before moving to my jeans, quickly unfastening them and searching for the condom. I couldn't find it. *Fuck.*

Her loud moans and quivering thighs told me she was coming. "Inside me, inside me." She stretched her arms, pulling any part of me she could reach.

"I can't find the damn condom," I whispered, kissing her stomach.

"Forget it. I'm on the pill."

That did it. I rose up and slammed into her. We both groaned loudly. She was hot and wet and so damn tight. My heels were pushing against the door as I pounded harder and faster into her, wrapping my arms around her small body as her inner muscles squeezed me again and again.

"Oh, yes," she cried, slim arms around my neck. Her tiny breasts bounced against my chest with each push.

It was so good. I covered her mouth, kissing her deeply as I felt my building release. Breaking away, a deep groan rolled from my throat as I hit it hard, my ass tightening as my cock jerked with each thrust, going off inside her. She pulled me tighter and wailed, rocking her pelvis. She was coming again, and I kept pushing. It had been a while since I'd had a good lay, and damn if this didn't feel like heaven. Her thighs were around my waist, and I didn't care if we were just supposed to be making out or sobering up or whatever the fuck we were doing. It was worth it.

Her trembling gradually subsided as did my thrusting, and my hands went lightly to her hips, sliding over her ass and up until I was resting on my forearms, my face hovering over hers. I kissed her cheek where that dimple hid, I kissed her chin, then I went back to her lips. Little by little, our breathing slowed. Her eyes blinked open, but she didn't speak. For a moment, she only studied my face. Then she lifted a finger and traced a light line from my forehead, down my cheek to my mouth.

That's when I saw the tears.

"Whoa, hey," I whispered, sitting up and pulling her with me, wrapping my arms around her and holding her against my chest. Her forehead dropped to my shoulder and I felt her jerking with sobs.

My chest tightened. I didn't know what to do with this. Why was she crying? "Did I hurt you?" I was still whispering. "I'm sorry, it's been a while. I was too rough—"

"No." She sniffed, shaking her head. Another jerky breath. "You were great. It was amazing." Then she broke again with a sob.

I was totally confused. "Then what?"

Her face lifted to mine, and the black eyeliner was running with the tears under her blue eyes. I cupped her cheeks in my hands and pushed the ugly tracks away with my thumbs. How could I make this stop?

She blinked and turned her face from mine. "It's nothing."

"Hell it isn't." My arms tightened around her, pulling her back. "Tell me."

"Oh, god, Patrick. You don't want to know."

"I do."

She paused a moment, still not looking at me, as if she were choosing her words. "It was," she hesitated. "It was the first time… The first time I've been with anyone. Since Blake."

Fuck. Okay, maybe I did want to know why she was crying, but shit. Now I didn't know what to do. We were quiet a moment, and I held her until her tears subsided. Then I tried a neutral approach.

"It was your first time in almost a year?"

She pulled off my lap and slid to the other side of the car, bending her knees to her chest. I looked to the windows, and the realization of where we were hit me fast.

"Let's go back to my place. We can't talk here."

She shook her head, looking out the glass. "I'd better go home."

Reaching for my shirt, I slipped it over her head. "You're spending the night with me."

"No," she tried to fight. "It's too much. I'm leaving next week, and I just… I had too much to drink is all."

"Fuck that. You're sleeping at my place." I pulled my jeans up. "No strings, fine. But you're not sleeping alone tonight."

She crossed her arms over her waist, and I reached for the seatbelt, pulling it across her shoulder and lap, and fastening it before climbing back to the front seat. We didn't speak the whole drive, but I glanced in the rearview mirror a few times. She continued gazing out the window, and I couldn't think of anything to say to make her feel better.

Finally, I had us in my parking garage. Helping her out, I gathered her shirt, tank, and bra all wadded into a roll, thanks to the way I'd removed them. She picked up her shoes and purse, still wearing my shirt over her jeans. Without her shoes, she seemed so small. Fragile.

"Come on," I said quietly, leading her to my door.

Inside, I dropped everything on the couch. I caught her swaying a few times, and took her hand. "Take your jeans off and just sleep in that shirt."

She nodded and bent down to remove her pants. I left her to go brush my teeth and find a shirt for me to sleep in. Moments later, we were in bed.

The idea of sex or making out was definitely off the table at this point, and all I knew to do was pull her to me. She didn't fight it, putting her cheek on my chest. I tried to think of something comforting to say, lying in the dark, smoothing her hair off her face, but only one thought was circling in my mind. It was stupid, and I said it anyway, softly, like a mantra. "Bee stings... needles... rope burns..."

"What?" Her voice was quiet, weary.

"When Stuart and I were kids we played this game. If one of us got hurt, we'd try and name things that hurt worse. It's stupid brother shit."

Tears were in her cracked whisper. "Nothing hurt like losing Blake."

My arms tightened around her, and I kissed the top of her head. "I know." My hand continued moving up and down her back. "Nothing kicks the shit out of you like love."

After that, I only held her. She didn't shake or jerk anymore with sobs, but I could tell she was still crying. I didn't know how much time passed before she stopped. I was struggling with sleep myself when she spoke again.

"This doesn't change anything." Her voice sounded like sleep, and my arms were still around her skinny body. I remembered the pizza I was supposed to buy her.

"Right," I said. "No strings. Just friends."

Then I thought of my kid sister Amy dealing with all Kenny had faced and being alone in some guy's bed. I would hope he wouldn't be a dickhead.

"You're safe here," I added. "Just sleep now."

In less than a minute, we were both out.

* * *

My eyes opened, and I was alone. Sitting up, I whipped the sheets back and grabbed my jeans off the chair before making my way down the hall to the kitchen. Where was she? Had she left?

"Kenny?"

"In the kitchen," she answered, and I saw her as I rounded the corner. She sat on the counter sipping coffee from a mug, looking even younger with no makeup and wearing my too-big shirt over her jeans. "I'm keeping this, by the way. It smells good—like you."

I shrugged, going over to lean beside her. "Sure."

She lowered her leg and hopped down, crossing the space to put her mug in the sink. I only watched her, wondering what to say. I didn't want to apologize—I wasn't sorry for what happened between us—but I wanted to know she was okay.

"I called a cab," she said. "It should be here any minute."

"Why did you do that? I'll drive you home."

"It's better this way." She returned to where I stood, pushing me back and leaning against my chest. Damn she was short without her stilts. I put my arms around her.

"You're good in bed." She said it like she was reading a weather report.

"So are you."

"If things were different, we'd definitely start dating now."

"But I thought—"

"And it would be a *huge* mistake, because we'd end up being each other's rebound person, and it would completely screw up this beautiful thing we've got here." She waved a finger back and forth between us.

My eyebrow cocked. "What do we have?"

"You helped me." A bony hip pushed against mine. Then her voice softened. "Thanks for that."

The forty-eight hours we'd known each other flew through my mind, from the first shot of those blue eyes to the dimple, the tattoo, last night in the car, her sleeping in my arms. I slid a dark lock off her cheek. "I hope I did."

"I put my number in your phone," she continued, stepping out of my arms. "Keep in touch, okay? Just as friends."

I nodded. "Are you feeling better today?"

"No. But I feel different."

I was going to say more, but the loud honking of the taxi horn broke up the moment. She reached down and grabbed her blue suede shoes then quickly stepped back to kiss my cheek before turning and dashing to the door. "You're a great guy, Patrick. Don't change because some stupid bitch screwed you over."

A smile crossed my lips. "And it's okay for you to start living again."

She nodded and made an air-kiss before heading out. I stood there thinking about what had happened. Dangerously sweet.

Picking up my phone, I scrolled to her number and typed a text. *Tell me if you ever need anything.*

Her reply flashed back. *Stop being so nice. Haven't you learned?*

I breathed a laugh. *Bye, Peg.*

*Bye, Bingley.*

## CHAPTER 4:
## SAFETY OFF

Bank fraud was the last thing on my mind as I sat at my desk Monday morning. All I could think about was Kenny. Not like I wanted her, although it was nice having her in my bed and definitely nice getting laid. Somehow, despite what happened in the car, my feelings changed through what happened between us to something different and new — to me, at least.

Rubbing my forehead, I realized she'd seen straight through me, and she'd managed to drag the real me out — the guy who could love someone enough to get hurt. Badly. I'd intended to keep that guy good and locked down. Maybe permanently.

She'd said we helped each other, but at the moment I was feeling shaken, off my game. Like I wasn't as hardened as I'd thought.

For Kenny and me, love had kicked both our asses, and in our own ways we'd shut it out, put up the walls, closed shop. I wasn't ready to reopen for business, but she'd put a crack in my barrier.

Now she was headed back to everyone who'd told her not to follow her heart in the first place. I wanted to go back with her—not as her boyfriend, more to punch anyone in the face who might try to say *I told you so.* I wanted to protect her from that. I wanted to protect us both.

It was a strange arrangement to love somebody I didn't want to screw—who wasn't my sister. Thankfully, Derek stopped at my door, interrupting all the cognitive dissonance bullshit.

"We hitting the gym this afternoon?" He was slightly less formal today—still in the suit, but no tie.

"Sure." I blinked back to my computer.

He stayed in my open door a beat longer. "Williams was impressed by your report Friday. If you're interested, I can give you the Alliance account."

"Thanks," I nodded. "I'll take it."

"Now I've got to straighten out this shit on my desk." He turned, and I heard him call Nikki in a tone that was sharper than usual. My brow lined. Even though she'd turned me down, Nikki was cool. I didn't like how he talked to her.

God, I was a gooey mess today. I had to fucking get it together.

She swished past my door, wearing a bright yellow wrap-dress. I shook my head and turned back to my computer. "Whatever," I said under my breath. Nikki was a big girl as she'd let me know.

Five minutes later, a loud slam had me out of my chair and into the hallway. Derek's door was the source of the noise, and inside Nikki was yelling. I couldn't believe my ears. For a few moments, I waited... this

52

wasn't exactly a domestic disturbance, but I knew from my training about walking in on these kinds of things. His door opened again, and I heard him speak.

"You need to calm down," he said in the sharp tone I knew from experience would get the exact opposite response. "I was just saying—"

"You were just implying I was incompetent. Again." I'd never seen Nikki mad, but her eyes were flashing as she spun back to her desk and snatched up her bag. From this angle, I could also see she was hurt. "You can do it yourself," she said loudly. "I quit."

My stomach dropped, and Derek and I both sprung forward at that.

"Wait—" I started.

"Stay out if it, Patrick," she snapped at me. "I've been here a lot longer than you, and I'm sick of his shit."

"Nikki, you're making a mistake." Derek used neither the tone nor the words I knew she wanted to hear. She wanted an apology.

"And you need to get laid." She spun on her heel and pushed through the glass doors. I caught a "Goodbye, Patrick" as the door breezed shut again.

Anger clear on my face, I turned back to my business partner. "The fuck?"

He shook his head and went back into his office. "I'll handle it," he said, slamming his dark wooden door.

For a moment, I stood there looking at her empty desk and his closed door. Princeton was supposed to be less drama. Shit.

\* \* \*

Derek stayed in his office with the door closed the rest of the day. I managed to get some work accomplished, but I was still restless by six. Going to the gym seemed like a good idea, although I figured I'd be going alone.

He emerged just as I was picking up my bag. Irritation rose in my chest, but I waited. "You coming?"

The phone rang in his office, and he held up a hand. "Meet you there in five."

Going back inside, he closed the door again, and I left for Building E ready to find out what happened in his office this morning.

At the gym, I loaded the bar with a more reasonable weight and lay back, lifting it myself and doing eight reps. Derek entered as I finished, and I returned it to the rack, sitting up to look at him.

He adjusted the strap on his glove and glanced at me briefly before picking up a set of dumbbells. I stood and went over to do the same, still not speaking.

"I talked to the temp service," he finally said. "New girl can start Friday."

I put the dumbbells on the rack roughly. "You're not getting Nikki back?"

He exhaled loudly and put his set down easier. "No."

At the bench-press bar, he added more plates to what I'd just done. Anger was rising in me with every one. "Why not?"

Then he paused and turned to me. "Patrick, you've been here a little more than a week. I get it you liked Nikki, or whatever was going on between you two, but she was a terrible secretary. She's lucky she stayed as long as she did."

He was giving me the little brother routine. Fuck that. I exhaled, jaw clenched. "Tell me what she did that was so bad. We're business partners. I should be in on decisions like this since they effect me."

"Fine," he sat up. "The day before you started, I had to fly to Manhattan. A quick, 24-hour trip, right?"

I shrugged. "Okay."

"She booked my flight in and out of JFK. She booked my car at LaGuardia." He let that sink in for a moment. "Do you know how far apart the two are?"

I crossed my arms. I didn't have a comeback.

"Between cabs and the hassle of getting in and out, I was late to all my meetings, I didn't get any work done. I fucking hate cabs."

"So she made a mistake. It's probably easy to do."

His brow furrowed. "You think?"

"Hell, I don't know. Maybe?"

"Okay, Thursday I've got to be in Dallas. I'm flying into Love Field. Do you know where my car was booked?"

My brow rose, and I almost laughed. "DFW?"

"Yes!" He exploded, and I did laugh. "It's a good thing I checked it today."

"Okay, so she sucks at travel plans." I picked up the towel, ready to let him have this one. "She types one helluva report."

"Nobody sees those but us." He tightened the strap on his glove. "She doesn't follow directions. I was supposed to have your portfolio on my last trip. It wasn't there. I'd made a digital presentation for the Wall Street guys. Not in my briefcase."

"But the police coding..." I couldn't resist.

"Don't give me that." He was still pissed, but at least I understood.

I walked over and pulled on the lat machine. "Well, I liked her," I said, catching the other handle.

"Maybe she needed more training."

Derek laid back and pushed on the bench-press bar. That's when I remembered I was supposed to be spotting and walked back over to him. "I don't have time to train a secretary," he grunted, pushing up. "I need someone I don't have to think for."

I helped him with his set, remembering the other part he'd said. "There wasn't anything between us. Not that I didn't try."

The muscle in his jaw moved, but he didn't answer.

"You gotta admit," I continued, "the girl was stacked."

He sat up, recovering. "No pens in the company ink," was his only response between breaths.

"Where else are you dipping it?"

"None of your fucking business."

I shrugged, picking up my towel and heading for the door. "Okay, but it's one thing to mourn somebody. It's another thing to give up. You're only forty."

"Thanks for the advice, Yolo."

"Exactly," I said before pushing through the door.

He continued with his workout, and I was pretty sure nothing I said had made a difference to him. Still it was worth a shot. I felt like Kenny would've wanted me to try.

* * *

The office was quiet with Nikki gone. I was between cases, restless and bored. I'd texted Kenny a few times, but she'd left for Bayville Tuesday afternoon. Derek took off for Dallas Thursday, and I was alone in the office, ready for anything to happen when I heard a little tap on my door.

Swiveling around in my chair, I felt my jaw drop, but closed it fast. *Hello, unspoken wish-fulfillment.* The woman in my doorway was tall with long, white-blonde hair and bangs that ended just in her dark brown eyes. She wore a tight beige dress with a *V* neck showing the right amount of cleavage, and all that awesome was perched on long, tanned legs ending in brown heels. In one blink, the distractions in my brain disappeared, and I remembered my new philosophy. New Patrick was back, and this female had his full attention.

"Are you Knight or Alexander?" Her voice was low and sultry, and her hand went to her hip, which cocked to the side. It was like a scene out of an old detective film. I half expected her to ask me for a cigarette.

"Patrick Knight," I said, rising. I held out my hand and gave her The Smile. "And you are?"

"Star Brandon." Her eyebrow rose in what seemed to be approval, and she put her cool hand in mine, holding it. No shake.

"Are you the new secretary?" I fucking loved our temp service. "I wasn't expecting you until tomorrow."

She released my hand, and her eyes traveled to my mouth then down my torso. I put my hands in my back pockets, letting my knit shirt stretch over my chest. Her expression never faltered.

"I just wanted to stop by and check out my new job."

"I understand." I didn't mind her checking out whatever she wanted. "Your desk is out there."

Her eyes returned to mine and she hesitated only briefly before turning on her heel and heading to the front. I followed, watching the nice sway of that ass in that dress. Things were getting better with every step.

"The laptop should be setup with everything you need," I said. "Honestly, Derek knows more about it than I do. He won't be back until Monday."

She pulled out a few drawers and studied the contents. Then she walked back around to where I stood. "What will we do tomorrow?" The way she said it almost sounded like a dare.

"If you just want to work a half-day, I won't mind."

Again, her eyes blinked up and down my torso. "Maybe we can take a long lunch."

"Maybe we can. It's a slow week, and we could get to know each other better."

"That's exactly what I was thinking, Mr. Knight."

"You can call me Patrick."

"And you can call me Star." A slow smile lifted her lips. "See you tomorrow."

I watched her walk out and leaned against the desk. Pens, ink, fuck it all. I was going there. Safety off.

## Chapter 5:
## You Only Live Once

Star's ass was absolutely gorgeous, smooth skin, lightly tanned. Her panties, if you could call them that, were just a thin, gold rope around the curve of her hips with a string running down the center line. I groaned and lay my head back against my chair as I watched her body move up and down in time with her head.

Smoothing her hair back from her face gave me the full view of her mouth sucking my dick. She dipped all the way down, taking me in, and then came back up, letting me pop out and giving me a wink. Her tongue licked around my tip like it was a fucking popsicle, then she wrapped those glossy lips around me and sucked again.

"Uhh," I groaned, sliding my fingers to her cheek. She was too good at this, and I was about to shoot. I fought the urge to move her head up and down with my hands. Humming noises came from her throat, and I groaned again as she slid her tongue down my length, her fingers massaging my balls.

"Fuck me," I hissed watching her make her way back to my tip, smoothing her tongue around it again as her hand quickly pumped my shaft. She blinked up at me and smiled, her tits lightly grazing my thighs, her nipples beaded. Then she ducked her head and took my whole cock into her mouth again, deep-throat. My ass clenched as I struggled to hold back.

"I'm about to come," I whispered, reaching for the condom. But she held my legs down and kept going. I was blacking out, it felt so good. "Star," I ground out. "I'm fucking about to come."

She sucked harder, still pumping my shaft fast with her hand as her mouth focused on my tip. Then she went all the way down again, and I blew. "Fuck!" I hissed as my cock jerked in her throat. She held on, swallowing, and my head dropped back against the chair as my back arched.

"Fucking… yes." I couldn't help holding her head then as I bucked against it, groaning. My stomach tightened, and I rocked my hips a few more times. Dammit, this girl was good. I rode out the last wave of that orgasm, and her mouth never left me.

Finally, I collapsed in my chair very satisfied. She sat back on her heels, wiping her lips with one hand and giving me a sideways grin. A little laugh came from her throat, and in my hazy afterglow, I smiled, studying her fine body, full tits, small waist, round hips with that gold-rope thong passing for panties wrapped over them.

"Good?" Her voice was a throaty purr.

"Yes, ma'am." My response was hoarse. "Very."

I tried to piece together how I'd lucked into this scenario—her naked in my office, on her knees, giving me a hummer for the record books.

This morning started innocent enough. Star was at her desk playing around on her laptop when I arrived. I smiled and greeted her before going back to my office to check emails and make sure nothing important was waiting. It wasn't.

Derek had emailed saying he'd be back on Monday to discuss "something big." He suggested I take the afternoon off as we might be working late for a few weeks. I walked back out front to see if Star still wanted to do lunch. She smiled and offered to get take-out for us to have in the conference room. It seemed like a good idea. I could give her the tour and answer any questions she might have about working here—as much as possible—then we could call it a day. Or whatever. I was flexible on that point.

Lunch had arrived, and when she went for drinks, she'd found the liquor supply we kept in the refrigerator for special occasions. A few vodkas later, she was slipping that tight black dress she wore slowly down her thighs, stepping out of it and undoing her bra to let those fine tits bounce out. Then she crossed the room to kneel in front of me. I didn't even try to stop her from undoing my fly. The memory of how it all came together had my cock stirring awake again.

"What should we do now?" She leaned forward, running both hands up my legs. I sat forward to meet her, sliding my hands up to cup her bare breasts.

"We've got take out in the conference room," I suggested, thinking of the lunch we never ate.

"Mmm..." She smiled that cat smile and pressed against my legs as I rolled her nipples between my fingers. I grew stiffer as she lifted the tumbler of vodka and took another long drink, giving me the full, up-close view of that body. "Or?"

"Or we could go out for drinks?" I glanced at the clock. It was already six, and I imagined hitting a bar then going back to my place for a nice, long night of her in my bed. With a start like this, no telling what all we might try. I was getting harder just thinking about it.

"Is that what you want to do right now?" Her eyes narrowed, and I was ready.

"Not really." I stood and lifted her by the upper arms, helping her turn around and lean forward over my desk on her stomach.

Her smooth, round ass was so pretty. Reaching forward, I took a long hit from my own vodka as I enjoyed the view a moment. Yes, this was nuts. I barely knew this woman, she was my employee...

It was also extremely fucking hot. The perfect office fantasy. *You only live once.*

I slid a finger under the center string of her thong, starting at her lower back and following it down then I moved my hand around to the front. She rested her cheek on the desk and whimpered when I found her clit through the thin fabric. Her breasts were pushed into full mounds beneath her, and I slid my fingers over the damp patch on her panties. Another sound came from her throat as I went beneath the fabric, lightly rubbing her swollen bud. Her ass swayed in front of me, and I opened the condom with my teeth, rolling it on one-handed.

"Oooh," she moaned as I massaged a little deeper, and her knees bent. I could tell she was getting there by the way her thighs were beginning to tremble. My fingers continued working her, and I kept my eyes on her ass. I moved the thin gold rope to the side and testing her opening. Hot and soaked.

"Oh, Patrick," she moaned again as my two fingers went inside her. I glanced up to see her eyes closed, and I removed my fingers, lifted my dick, and with one hard push, I was in — tight, wet and welcoming. I groaned loudly. Pussy was the greatest gift.

Keeping my fingers on her clit, my other hand gripped her waist. I was ready to rock her til she begged me to stop, but she pushed up on the desk against me, arching her back and matching my strength.

"Fuck," I groaned as she reached for my thighs, still banging against me. I sat back in the chair, and she never broke contact.

Now she was on my lap, leaning forward against the desk with me full inside her. My hands were on her hips and her hand had replaced mine between her legs. She bounced up and down, and I could see the reflection of her tits in the window, doing the same as she got herself off on my lap. I clutched her waist feeling my own explosion coming.

"Oh, god, Oh, yes!" She was riding me hard and fast, reverse cowgirl, and I leaned back and enjoyed the show, feeling her inner muscles tightening around me, seeing her juices coming down, covering me. I wanted to let her finish, but damn this was too much, even for me. My ass tightened as the pressure built…

"Fuck," I yelled as I shot off. I held her against me and stood, pushing her forward onto the desk so I could slam her hard. This was more than hot. It was fucking awesome.

Her brow clutched as her mouth opened wide. Then she wailed, pushing back against me, and I managed to shoot off a little more as she finished. I was pretty sure I saw stars, and I laughed, wondering if that was how she got her name. It was very possible I was a little drunk. Maybe more than a little.

Sliding her hair off her back, I kissed her between the shoulder blades. Her body moved with her laugh, and I ran my hand down her back, pulling out and disposing of the condom.

I studied her with a satisfied smile as I pulled up my pants. "I'm about one hundred percent sure I'll only be thinking of one thing when I sit at this desk now."

She rose and walked to where she'd left her dress in a puddle at my door. Facing me, she again gave me the full view of her body as she slowly slid it up her legs. "Maybe you need a private secretary," she said with a wink.

"I like that idea." I buttoned my shirt as I watched her.

Just then her phone buzzed. It was still on my desk from where she'd left it after ordering the takeout. I glanced over and saw the name *Tom Brandon* flashing on the screen, and my eyebrows pulled together. *Brandon.*

My brain was fuzzy from our vodka lunch with a side of multiple orgasms, but a warning instinct went off low in my stomach.

"Who's—" I started, but she jerked her dress over her shoulders and snatched the phone off my desk.

That told me more than I wanted to know. Forcing my brain to focus, I stood and caught her arm, pulling her back and turning the phone in her hand so I could see the face. Her eyes blinked nervously to me as she tried to move away, but I held her fast.

"Are you married?" Anger flared in my chest, pushing out any good feelings I might've had just moments ago.

"We're separated," she said with a nervous laugh. "I don't know why Tommie's calling me."

"The fuck?" I backed away trying to shake the fog out of my head. A husband? "You're married and you were in here..." What kind of fucked up shit had I stepped in?

She lunged forward then, grabbing my arm. Long nails cut into my skin, and I snapped it away. "Don't look at me like that," she hissed, eyes flashing.

"How am I supposed to look? You should've said you were married."

"Yeah? Before or after you stuck your dick in my mouth?"

*Shit.* Now I was pissed. My jaw clenched, and a thought flashed across my brain, I was the fucker in 24B. Shaking that away, I studied her posture. Defensive, ready to fight. I had to sober up fast and solve this problem before it all went to hell.

"Look," I said, softening my voice and fighting back what I really wanted to say. "Why don't we call it a day, and you can check in with him."

Her brown eyes studied my expression, waiting. I did my best to give her a warm smile. Not The Smile as I was already in a shitload of shit as it was.

"Okay," she said. "I'll call you when I get home."

How the fuck did she have my number? The cold realization that she had access to everything as the office secretary washed over me. Great. That was all I needed, some damned *Fatal Attraction* bullshit. Next thing I knew, she'd be boiling bunnies.

"Sounds great," I said, doing the acting job of my life. She needed to stay calm, and I needed a break to sober up and figure this out.

I leaned forward and kissed her cheek. Her head turned as if she was trying to meet my lips, but I wasn't kissing that. I stepped back and slid my hand down her arm to squeeze hers. "See you Monday."

"Monday?" Dark brows pulled together under those white-blonde bangs. "But I thought we might do something before then."

Anger, frustration, anger again... My whole body was tense, but I smiled casually. "It's just I've got this... Uh, I might have to go out of town." The idea of visiting Kenny for the weekend crossed my mind.

Her bottom lip pushed forward into a pout that I might've thought was sexy. Like five minutes ago. Now I just wanted to get the hell out of here.

"Let me know if your plans change," her voice was higher, but it still had that husky undertone.

"I will," I said, leaning forward to grab my keys and my phone off the desk. It was no use locking my office or trying to protect anything. I'd already given her the master key. *Fuck.* "Just lock up when you leave, okay?"

She nodded, her eyes following me out. I skipped the elevators, and instead slowly backed through the metal doors of the stairwell, still smiling and waving as she watched me through the glass entrance to our office.

Once I was out of sight, I took the steps two at a time. Jumping the last flight, I burst out the bottom door, quickly making my way to the Charger and punching up Kenny's number.

## Chapter 6:
## Fucking Fatal Attraction

*MFGDMFS!* I typed and hit Send before backing out of my parking space.

I didn't look out my window, but I could feel Star watching me from the offices above. I'd seriously screwed the pooch this time — in every sense of the word. And I was pissed as hell. My phone vibrated and I glanced at it.

*LOL, WTF?* Kenny texted back.

I waited for the next red light and answered. *Any chance I can crash with you this weekend?*

The light changed, and I dropped the phone on the passenger's seat. My brain was working out all the possible scenarios. Star knew where I lived, and judging by her behavior just now, I was pretty confident she'd be stalking me this weekend. But how far would she go? My grip tightened on the steering wheel. I'd never get any sleep worrying about having to fight off some knife-wielding crazybitch in the middle of the night.

Kenny texted back: *Only if you can figure out what to tell my parents.*

Fuck. I pulled into my parking garage and replied: *You don't have your own place?*

*How much money do you think I make, Bingley?*

Shit. That plan was out. I slammed the car door and jogged up the few flights of stairs to my place. My brain felt scrambled, and I was tired. I needed to lay low for a few days and figure this out. Pressing my lips together, I figured I could rent a hotel room somewhere in town… I considered the other *what if* as I unlocked my apartment. What if I was overreacting?

Just because Star was screwing around on her husband didn't mean she was a psycho. Yes, her words in my office and that crazy-assed look in her eyes were not encouraging signs, but I could be wrong about the whole thing.

*What's going on?* Kenny texted.

For a moment, I only stared at my phone, thinking. Then I typed it. I figured Kenny's response would give me a good idea what to expect.

*I might've fucked Fatal Attraction.*

*LOLOL!!!* She texted back.

*Thanks.*

Actually, her laughter gave me the tiniest bit of hope Derek might see the humor in this situation as well, however slight. Then my mind scrolled through all the possible ramifications of what I'd done, and I felt sick all over again. Nope. He'd be pissed.

*Sorry. Are you really in trouble?*

*I'll be OK.* I answered. *Don't worry.*

*Now I'm worried.*

*Don't. I'm handling it.*

I dropped the phone on my bed and went straight to the shower. I wanted to wash, no scrub this day off me. I wished I had a brillo. Turning the water on hot, I waited until the thin, white steam started to rise before I stepped inside and laid it all out in my mind.

Problem number one: Star was a subordinate, which meant she could claim sexual harassment and sue me. Whether it was true or not, the publicity would kill us. Derek was going to kick my ass. And I deserved it.

Problem number two: Star's husband. Was he crazy? Did he own a gun? Would he show up at the office threatening to use it? Again, Derek was going to kill me. I had to fix this.

Then a new potential problem hit me. If this shit got out of hand before Sunday, I had no backup. Maybe I should just tell Derek now and ask if I could crash at his place for a few nights. That option made my stomach burn.

I decided to think about it more before pulling that trigger. It was possible once Derek returned on Monday, Star would take one look at him and drop it. "Mr. Alexander" was a pretty intimidating force in the office, and he ran a tight ship. Maybe I could slowly disengage.

Washing my hair, giving my body and particularly my dick an extra good scrubbing, I stepped out feeling calmer. I wrapped the towel around my waist and noticed the face of my phone was covered in texts. Picking it up, my adrenaline started pumping again. Sixteen texts. One from Kenny, fifteen from Star.

Kenny: *Check in, okay?*
Star #1: *You there?*
#2: *Patrick?*
#3: *Please text back. I'm worried.*

#4: *I miss you already.*
#5: *When I move, I can tell you've been inside me.*
Fuck.
#6: *I can still taste you.*
Double Fuck.
#7: *Do you miss me?*
#8: *Why aren't you texting me back?*
#9: *Where are you?*
#10: *Are you avoiding me?*
#11: *You know you can't avoid me.*
#12: *I see your lights on.*

Fuck Fuck Fuck! I resisted the urge to slam my phone into the wall and instead read her last three messages.

#13: *I'm waiting here til you text back.*
#14: *Patrick?*
#15: *I'm coming up.*

The thought of no backup again crossed my mind, and I decided to vacate the premises. Tossing my towel on the bed, I jerked on my jeans and a maroon tee. I stepped into a pair of loafers, and snatched my keys off the front counter, slipping out the door and locking it behind me. The lights were still on, but that would add to my story — I'd forgotten to turn them off before I left.

Last thing I wanted was to run into Star, so I used my stealth training. Creeping down the breezeway, I went opposite my normal route. With my back to the wall, I edged down to the parking garage. Not seeing anyone, I went car by car until I was at the Charger and jumped inside, jamming the key in the ignition and turning it. This whole scenario was pissing me off even more, but when I turned the wheel, I saw a dark figure exiting the garage in the direction of my apartment. Dammit. Now I'd have to tell Derek.

There was no way to know if she'd seen me. Well, I could wait for the texts to start pouring in, but I was scrolling through my contacts first. When I saw his name, I took a deep breath and touched the screen. A few buzzes later, and he answered.

"Patrick?" Derek's voice held a note of confusion. "Is something wrong?"

"Hey, man." I switched to casual cool. "Need to ask a favor if possible."

"Okay…"

There was a brief pause, and I thought about my story. He was going to be pissed as hell, so I decided to let him finish what he was doing and tell him the truth in person when he got back.

"Seems they were doing some maintenance in my building today, and the power was knocked out. Still is."

I heard him exhale. "That sucks."

"Yeah," I said. "It's probably too much to ask, but would you mind if I crashed at your place tonight?"

"Sure." A smile was in his voice. That wouldn't last long. "Stay as long as you need. I'll call the manager and have the doorman let you in."

"Thanks, D. I owe you one."

"No worries."

I ended the call and turned the wheel toward downtown. It was possible Star might figure out where I'd gone, but with valet parking, a gated garage, and a doorman, I'd at least have three layers between me and the crazy. And I'd bet my life Derek Alexander didn't have any female visitors that looked like her. Although, now that I thought about it, he could do whatever he wanted, and I'd never know. Nah, he wouldn't have been as quick to let me crash at his pad if he were hiding a secret double-life.

By the time I reached the glass doors at the entrance of his building, the doorman and valet were waiting for me. There was something to be said about luxury living. Maybe in a few years, I'd look into a similar arrangement.

"Good evening, Mr. Knight," the doorman said, glancing briefly at my ID. "This won't be necessary next time."

"Thanks... Walter," I said, reading the man's small, gold nameplate. "I'll only be here a day. Two tops."

"Enjoy your visit, sir," he said with a smile.

I nodded and started for the elevator, but then I stopped. "Oh, Walter—"

"Yes, sir?" He stepped back to me.

"I'm not expecting *any* visitors."

"Of course." He nodded, and I smiled.

"Thanks."

He returned to his post, and I entered the waiting elevator, collapsing against the back wall as the doors slid closed.

* * *

Standing at the dark windows overlooking the lights of Princeton, I let out a deep exhale. I was tired. I'd been drinking since lunch, I'd had no lunch... I'd fucking fucked through lunch—all followed by that insane adrenaline trip from hell. Now I was looking back over the whole thing, growing more and more pissed. Mostly at myself.

I'd sent Kenny a short text that I was at Derek's, and after her smartass response about hiding, I'd silenced my phone after Text #50 from Star. My head hurt, and I couldn't believe I'd been such an amateur.

Walking through Derek's plush condo, I debated how I could present this in a way that didn't end up with all signs pointing to me applying for one of those Afghanistan jobs.

The condo was noticeably free of any photos or personal mementos. It was like a fucking museum. At twenty-five hundred square feet, it wasn't warm or homey. The décor reminded me of the office with its dark wood and spare furnishings. Glass and stainless, granite and all the latest appliances. The beds were plush with 800 thread-count sheets and those firm but soft mattresses. I think they were the Swedish kind. Of course, they were. This was Mr. Alexander.

It was a dream living space, but it was clear the two-bedroom, two bath condo was just that — a living space. Nikki was right. My partner seriously needed to get laid, but I was pretty sure if I suggested anything like that to him on the heels of my latest fuckup, I'd be the one getting punched in the face.

Digging around in the freezer, I fished out a bottle of Belvedere and poured two fingers into a crystal tumbler. There wasn't much food in the condo, so I called for take out. Not only was I tired, I was *hangry* — hungry *and* angry.

I felt conned. I felt trapped. My food-deprived brain plotted out all sorts of scenarios. What if Star was a plant from some angry client I'd sent away? Some client who knew my weakness for hot blondes and blow jobs.

Or possibly she was a setup by Nikki intended for Derek, and I'd unwittingly intercepted her. No way. Nikki was smarter than that, whatever my senior partner said. He'd never fall for it. That thought made me fucking pissed at myself all over again. It would be the first thing he said.

Once I'd eaten a boatload of sushi, I was thinking a little clearer. Yes, I'd screwed up. It was a slow day, and I'd been thinking with my dick instead of my brain. And it was biting me in the ass. Now I needed to figure out a way to smooth this over that didn't involve us getting sued for sexual harassment or me having to take out a restraining order against some jealous ex-husband. If he even was her ex. My instincts told me they were still together. Where were my instincts around one o'clock this afternoon?

Standing, I went back to the windows and looked out at the darkness, broken by streetlights, cars, and smaller businesses. How had I ended up here? I'd left Chicago determined to change how I did things, but my anger at Stacy had left me out of control. It was a dangerous place to be; *out of control* in my line of work was a career killer. I was the watcher, the thinker. The closer. And here I was committing frat-boy fuckups with would-be porn stars. Something had to give.

My phone vibrated in my hand, and I was so distracted, I looked at it. Kenny. *Don't beat yourself up, Bingley. I've seen you. You've got that dangerously sweet charm.*

Allowing myself a momentary reprieve from the self-flagellation, I thought of Kenny and me. Being with her was really nice. For one night I'd felt calm.

If only she wasn't such a kid. I shook my head. Her circumstance had morphed all my feelings into nothing more than big-brother protectiveness.

*I was actually just awarding myself King Dumbass.* I texted back.

*You are a dumbass. But you're not the king. And Darcy is more understanding than he first appears.*

Her intuition made me laugh. *Thanks.*

Warmth filled my chest, even if it was the warmth I usually reserved for relatives like my little sister. Kenny was special. And all I could do now was wait.

## Chapter 7:
## Back in the Desert

Watching the anger rise in Derek's face reminded me of the day I decided he could probably be one scary-assed motherfucker if he wanted to be. I was absolutely correct in that assessment. Not only did his blue eyes turn dark navy, but his brow lowered in a way that had my muscles tensing, preparing to take the hit. It was going to hurt like hell, too. I'd seen him work out.

"You did *what*?" His voice was quiet, way more controlled than I'd expected.

My stomach was tight. "I made a mistake."

"A mistake?" He let out his breath and turned, looking through the windows of his apartment at the bright Sunday afternoon. "A mistake is Nikki sending my car to LaGuardia instead of JFK. This is more than a mistake."

The comparison made me wince. I'd spent the weekend at his place, worked out on his Bowflex, lounged by the rooftop pool, watched his 110-inch flatscreen, tried to get my head straight. The more I'd thought about what happened, the more it didn't make sense that Star would go from zero to on my dick unless she had an agenda. Sure, I'd grown used to panties flying at my command, but this felt contrived.

"What do you think about it possibly being a setup?" It sounded even more ridiculous when I said it out loud, and even if it was a setup, it didn't change the fact that I'd slept with a subordinate. On her first day in the office.

As if remembering something, Derek turned and went to the hall, grabbing his briefcase. "With what possible motive?" He was distracted as he walked past me. I couldn't imagine what he was looking for—unless he had standard resignation papers on hand.

"That's the part I can't figure out." I exhaled, leaning against his leather couch. "But I swear, I was only planning to have lunch with her then go home. I'd gotten your email."

"Instead, you decided to jeopardize the reputation of our agency—my reputation—to satisfy your dick." Again I winced as he dropped the folder on the table. "You're going to Scottsdale. Leaving Tuesday morning. Take Monday off."

I nodded, expecting as much.

"Perfect timing," he growled. "I just picked up a huge multi-agency phishing scam targeting seniors. I need you on this. Instead, I've got to figure out if we're going to be sued for sexual harassment. Or if some asshole's going to show up at the office waving a gun."

My frown deepened. I still couldn't believe I'd been so careless. "I guess it's too late to apologize."

"Skip it," he said, picking up his phone. "I'll call Susan and see if the girl's reported anything."

"Who's Susan?"

"My aunt." He walked back to the dining area. "She runs the temp agency."

That one sentence made my setup theory DOA. Derek's aunt would not be party to a setup. I watched as he listened and then put his phone down. "She's not answering. I'll follow up with her tomorrow. You get packing."

I bent down and collected the few things I'd brought with me Friday night. I wasn't sure what to say in my defense at this point. My credibility was at an all-time low, and I hated it. I nodded, picking up my keys and my now-quiet phone. "Thanks."

"I'll email you the agenda for the Scottsdale conference. It's at the Windsor. Nice golf course, spa attached. Try the acupuncture."

"Right," I said, shaking my head. With the extra-sharp needles, I was sure. "See you in a week."

Maybe a week in the desert was a good idea after all.

* * *

Two days later, I was at the outdoor bar at the Windsor resort, waiting for a bartender and watching the Arizona sky turn from orange and pink to purple and black. I was alone, and I contemplated being here, in the desert, starting over. I had my agenda for the week, and the plan was to bag at least five new clients as penance. This was me grabbing the reins, getting back in the saddle.

Out of the blue, Derek had emailed to say he was joining me on the trip. Something about a last-minute job and needing to be here. He'd arrived earlier this evening, but I wasn't interested in socializing. This trip was about me redeeming my reputation.

And just like that, a vodka and tonic appeared in front of me. "From the lady." The bartender pointed past me to a strawberry blonde with a sly smile on her face. She was slim and fit, and I could tell by the way she carried herself, she was older.

Damn, if this wasn't a test.

I'd been with a few cougars after Stacy, and they were all crazy in the sack. They were experienced, confident, and usually not looking for anything long-term. Naturally, I felt a stirring down below, but I wasn't getting sidetracked. My dick might be awake, but he was taking the backseat on this trip. I nodded and lifted the tumbler mouthing a thank you.

She slid off that stool and headed in my direction. Shit. The filmy black dress she wore moved over her slim hips like smoky sex. Yep, a challenge.

"Hey, handsome," she said, holding out her hand. "I'm Barbara."

"Patrick." I gave it a squeeze, and she leaned against the bar in front of me.

Up close, she was even prettier. High cheekbones, bright hazel eyes with faint lines in the corners, and the sharp features that came with maturity. The little guy below was shooting all kinds of messages to my brain, but I was ignoring them.

"Are you here for the banker's conference?" Barbara signaled the bartender before turning back to me.

"As a matter of fact I am. You?"

She shook her head before ordering a glass of Chardonnay. "My youngest daughter's getting married tomorrow. I'm just in for the night." Following an obvious glance at my left hand, she gave me a wink before continuing. "Any plans for this evening, Patrick?"

Trust me, I'd already checked for rings on her fingers as well—burn me once—but none of that mattered. "Just finishing my drink here—thanks again—then headed up."

"Alone? Haven't you heard the expression, 'All work and no play'?" She made a pretend-scolding face before the smile returned. Her hazel eyes sparkled, a cool ivory hand slipped that almost-red hair off her shoulder. It was a very nice shoulder.

Yes, sometimes it was just that easy, dammit. "I've been living by it. In reverse. Now I've got to make amends."

"And how are you planning to do that?"

It took all my will-power to say it. "All work and all work. And my timing feels particularly shitty at this moment."

"I'll say. Are you sure you won't make an exception?"

"I can't believe I'm saying no." Standing, I signaled the bartender and then passed over two bills. "For this and whatever else she'd like."

Then I squeezed her arm gently, leaning forward to kiss her cheek. "I'm willing to bet you'll be prettier than the bride tomorrow," I whispered next to her ear.

She shook her head, but I knew I was leaving her happy—no harm, no foul, my resolve intact. And now I was headed back to my room, pissed off dick and all.

One of the best parts of being sent to Scottsdale was all the beautiful women on relaxing spa vacations, but I steeled myself. I had to redeem my reputation with Derek and by extension Stuart. I didn't want to hear any big-brother bullshit about how I'd screwed up a gig he'd dropped in my lap, or how I'd lost my girl and lost my edge. I'd done great work handling the Alliance case, and I was following it up with more great work. When I returned from this trip, I intended to be too valuable to lose.

\* \* \*

Two nights down, and two highly productive mornings were under my belt. I'd landed analysis meetings with five financiers once we got back, two of which were big-wig corporate-banking types, and I'd picked up cards from five more I'd touch base with post-con. I was moving back to the top of my game. The Closer, getting it done.

Derek texted last night. We were meeting for a recon in the fitness center before lunch. I was freaking walking on air and feeling more in control than ever. My confidence was even restored about handling the Star situation. A week of distance, a return to normal office behavior, and we could put what happened behind us. Or work out a financial settlement.

The same was not true of my senior partner. I didn't know what, but something was off with him. For starters, he hadn't overloaded the bench press bar. He didn't even seem to be paying attention to what I was lifting. Granted, I'd only known the guy a month, but I'd never seen him so distracted. I did a full set of eight reps and then guided the bar back to the rack—without my spotter's help.

Sitting up, I threw the towel around my neck. "You going to tell me what's up?" I asked after several quiet moments.

He blinked to me as if coming out of a daze. "Sorry, what?"

I watched him pick up the dumbbells and slowly curl one then the other. It was half the weight he normally used.

"What's the case you're working on?" I picked up my water bottle and went over to where he stood, studying his expression. I couldn't put my finger on what was different, but he seemed more relaxed somehow. Possibly happier, definitely troubled.

He put the weight down and went over to sit on the bench. "Domestic case," he said, not meeting my eye.

"I thought we didn't do those." I put my stuff aside and lifted a dumbbell.

He wasn't working out, and I was ready to finish my set and get lunch. I'd been up since eight sitting through meetings, and I wanted to spend the afternoon by the pool or possibly hitting the links.

"It's for a fellow I used to know," he said. "But I'm not sure I can help him now."

Again, I heard that tone in his voice, like he was surprised. Or bewildered. I couldn't put my finger on which.

"Can I help?"

He glanced up at me, then stood. "I can handle it. Things just got more complicated than I expected."

"Hey," I threw my towel at his head, hoping to snap him out of it. "Meet me at the Bluefin Grill for lunch. We can talk about it. And about what's going on back at the office."

"Sure," he said, folding the towel and setting it aside.

Something was definitely off with Mr. Control. But if I'd been sent to the desert to get my head straight, there was no reason he couldn't do the same.

## CHAPTER 8:
## BROKEN RULES

It was only Day Three. My massive screw-up waiting back at the office was still hanging over my head. My focus on work and building clients was still top priority on my mind. And in walked Elaine Merritt like a stealth bomb straight to the heart.

Derek had gone up to shower, and I was supposed to be getting us a table at the restaurant. I gave my name to the hostess and stepped over to the huge aquarium to wait, and just like that, she walked right up to me and introduced herself.

All she had on was a green sundress and flip-flops. I'm pretty sure she wasn't even wearing makeup, but everything about her hit me hard, from her perky nose to her bright green eyes to her shiny blonde hair. I couldn't take my eyes off her.

Still, I fought it. "All work and all work." That was the plan.

"Are you here for the convention?" It was the same question Barbara had posed, but the words were a thousand times more tempting coming from Elaine's soft lips.

Her voice was clear and confident, and with the slightest hint of playfulness. *Shit.* I almost said *No. Clearly, I came here to meet you*, but I calmed those thoughts.

"Yeah," I said, finding my control. "Are you?"

"We're here for the spa."

The term *we*, prompted me to look behind her where I noticed a pretty brunette holding back. She was clearly not interested in socializing, but I greeted her anyway. Elaine introduced her as her best friend Melissa, and I tried to be polite, but my focus was drawn back to the glowing nymph in front of me. I asked them to join us for lunch, and I could tell Elaine was interested by the way she looked at me. Melissa blocked it with some excuse, so I went for dinner. *Yes.*

I handed her my business card, and her eyes briefly moved from my hand to my torso and up my chest. Then she realized I'd caught her checking me out, and the faintest pink touched her cheek. Gorgeous.

A flicker of my first meeting with Kenny crossed my mind — the sweet blush, the curiosity. But again, everything was different with Elaine. For starters, she was closer to my age, and what I was feeling was not brotherly. I knew exactly what I wanted from this woman.

They were gone when Derek finally joined me for lunch. We decided to sit at the long bar that ran in a curvy circle around the center of the restaurant rather than at a table, and I couldn't help sweeping the room for her before we sat. No luck.

"I almost started without you," I said as the bartender put large club sandwiches in front of each of us.

Bacon spilled out of mine, which I immediately scooped up with my fingers into my mouth, getting a salty-tangy blast. Then I snagged a thick-cut French fry off my plate and shoved it in my mouth.

"Sorry," he said. "I was answering emails."

I nodded, chewing, waiting. "So spill it," I finally said. "Why are you acting like you just robbed the hotel safe?"

Derek reached for the glass of water sitting on the glossy bar in front of him and took a long sip, not meeting my eyes. For a few moments he didn't answer. Then he only said, "Something happened."

"Something like what?" I asked between bites.

"I've crossed some pretty significant lines, and I'm not sure how to handle it."

That stopped me. If I'd learned anything in the last month, it was Derek Alexander did not cross lines. I also noticed he wasn't eating. Something major must've happened, but his tone didn't match what he was saying. It didn't add up. His words were serious, but his voice was… happy?

"What have you done?" I asked, preparing to troubleshoot.

"I can't say. But I'm pretty sure it's your fault somehow." He actually smiled, and took a bite of his lunch then.

*What the hell?* I leaned back on the stool, frowning. "I'm not taking the blame for anything until I know what it is."

He put the sandwich down and clapping me hard on the shoulder. "Just know it's a good thing." Then his voice dropped, and his eyes returned to his drink. "Once I figure it out, I think it's going to be a very good thing."

He seemed finished discussing his mysterious problem, and I took another bite, thinking about my not-so-mysterious problem. "So what's happening back at the office?"

Derek took another sip of the water before answering. "Haven't caught up with Susan yet," he said. "I left a message for her to have our new secretary close up shop for the week. Told her we had a pretty big, unexpected case come up and not to worry about coming in. But we'd still pay her for the time."

"Think that'll work?"

"With no one there to train her or give her assignments, there's no reason for her to go in. Try not to worry about it. As soon as I catch up with Sue, we'll work out some plan for getting a replacement."

I nodded. "At least the texts have stopped."

"Hopefully this will just be a somewhat stressful learning experience for you." He shocked me by smiling again, then he stood and put his napkin on the bar. "I've got to do some work. See you later."

"At eight." I stopped him. "I made dinner dates for us. Be back here at eight."

"What?" I couldn't figure this guy out. Now he seemed angry. Whatever. He'd get over it when he saw Melissa. She was pretty hot, if somewhat quiet.

"Two very lovely ladies I met before you came down are joining us for dinner. Trust me, you'll like them."

His lips pressed into a frown. "Are they here for the convention?"

"They're here for the spa."

Something flickered in his eyes, like vague disbelief. "The spa?" He nodded, saying, "I'll be here," before taking off again.

"At eight," I repeated, my thoughts already skipping ahead to tonight and seeing Elaine again.

\* \* \*

Dinner could not have gone better if I'd planned every second. Elaine and Melissa showed up just minutes after Derek and I'd taken our seats, and after some strange hesitation on Melissa's part, we all were sitting and sharing glasses of cava. I wouldn't have ordered the Spanish sparkling wine, but Derek's choice turned out to be exactly right for the evening. Elaine's eyes shone along with the crystal and the drinks. Everything about her was radiant and beautiful. She was amazing. Her lips parted, and I wanted to taste those lips. I wanted to hold her in my arms. I wanted her in my bed.

"So what do you do to be so buff?" She asked, touching my bicep.

"We're private investigators," I said, catching her hand and holding it. She didn't pull away. "And we've done complete background checks on both of you lovely ladies."

It was a joke, I didn't even know her last name, which she was quick to point out.

"Liar!" she cried with a laugh, and if I weren't already into her, I'd have fallen then.

At that moment, Melissa stood and excused herself. I hadn't been paying attention to the other end of the table. She'd been talking quietly to Derek, and I couldn't imagine he'd said anything to upset her.

"Is something wrong?" I asked.

"I'm just not feeling well," she said, holding out her hand. "I'll have dinner in the room. Please stay and finish your meal."

"You don't have a key!" Elaine was instantly out of her chair, and my stomach dropped. My night with her could not end so soon, but of course, she had to go after her friend. *Shit*. Melissa hurried out, and we were all on our feet. But Derek saved my night. He touched Elaine's arm.

"I'll check on her," he said. "Stay and enjoy your dinner."

"But…" Elaine looked at him for a moment and then in the direction her friend went. Her brow pulled together and she studied him a moment. "I don't know…"

"I'll make sure she gets back safely."

She nodded briefly, and he took off faster than I'd ever seen him move. I didn't care, the only thing I wanted was for Elaine to sit down again and not worry.

"He's retired Marine," I said with a grin. "You know how those guys are."

Her green eyes flickered back to mine, and her face relaxed into that beautiful smile. "Always has to be the first on the scene?"

"That's the motto," I said, hoping to ease her mind. "He'll be sure she's okay. Trust me, he's a good guy."

"And I'll check on her in a few minutes," she said, lifting her glass.

We each took another sip of cava, and she rested her cheek on her hand. "How long have you two been partners?"

"Only about a month." I placed my arm on the back of her chair. "But my older brother was his business partner for years before me."

She sat up straighter when our waiter appeared. I ordered a steak, and Elaine asked for whatever the spa selection was for dinner. The fellow left, and she turned back to me.

"Were you a Marine, too?" Her eyes traveled to my lips, then to my chest, and finally back to her hand resting on the table.

"National Guard." Leaning forward, I slid my fingers under hers. "My brother was a major jarhead all during high school. He signed up the minute they let him in, but I only planned to get money for college. Of course, we both were sent overseas."

Her laugh came as easily as her smile, and my thoughts traveled ahead to when I might have a chance to kiss her.

"What was that like?" she asked.

"It was actually a lot better than I expected. I liked the teamwork, the friendships, the rush. It can be addictive. Stuart keeps going back."

"Are you here to stay?"

Studying her lovely face, I didn't say *definitely*. "When I started with Derek, it was that or going back. But I'm ready to focus on my life here."

Our dinner arrived, and the server put a plate with leaf salad, couscous, cashews, and what looked like beets in front of Elaine. I had a filet mignon, asparagus, and baked potato, and I caught her eyes drifting longingly to my dish.

Once the waiter was satisfied we didn't need anything more, I leaned forward. "What the hell did you order?"

Her loud laugh was unexpected and awesome. I fell a little bit more, if that was even possible, as she quickly put her slim hand over her mouth. "I'm sorry!" she said, shaking her head. "I was thinking the same thing!"

I couldn't help but laugh, too. "What is it?"

"I think this is what they call *raw foods*," she said, finally regaining some control. "Isn't it the worst? We've been getting it all week."

"Are you on a diet?" I cut a thick slice of steak and studied her trim waist before putting it in my mouth. It was perfectly cooked, slightly salty, and had the texture of velvet.

She shook her head and stirred the couscous with her fork. "It's part of the spa regimen. Cleansing or something."

I put my fork down. "You're not going to eat that."

Her guilty expression told me she just might. "I had a hamburger and fries for lunch," she whispered. "Melissa and I sneaked out."

Picking up my knife, I cut another thick portion of steak and slipped it onto her platter of rabbit food. "Have some of this. They'll never know."

"You're a bad influence." She bit her bottom lip before forking the steak and putting it in her mouth. Then she leaned back and groaned. "That's amazing!"

"I might enjoy watching you eat my steak more than having it myself."

"I'll help you decide." She scooted closer, and I was ready to pass my plate to her.

"We'll split it," I said.

Her soft blonde hair spilled around her shoulders, which were bare in the strapless dress she wore, and I thought of a half-dozen other ways to get that groan from her again. Fun ways.

The rest of dinner was spent discussing her work as a middle school English teacher, a profession I still couldn't envision her doing.

"Sixth graders are the best," she said, her eyes drifting thoughtfully. "Seventh is the most challenging."

"More than eighth?"

"Yes. Eighth graders are getting ready for high school, they're nervous and sentimental... Seventh is like the middle-child years. Lots of attention-grabbing."

We finished my steak in half the time, and I sat back, enjoying the wine and lightly touching the skin on her upper arm as my hand rested on the back of her chair. She leaned toward my touch, and I was ready to ditch the bright, white dining room for something more intimate.

"Let's take a walk," I said, signing the bill.

"Oh, you didn't have to pay for dinner!" She reached for me, but I caught her hand, lacing our fingers. "I'm not letting you pay for that plate of... whatever it was."

"Raw foods." She picked up a peppermint as we stood.

Our hands parted as she led the way through the restaurant, and all I could think of was touching her again. I hadn't been able to stop finding ways to touch her the entire meal, but she didn't seem to mind. Actually, I'd noticed her touching me the few times my hand left her.

When we were finally outside the restaurant in the wide hall leading to the conference center, she stepped toward me, catching the crook of my arm. I pulled her close and led us out the side door into the warm night. A wide path ran around the perimeter of the golf course near the hotel, and I knew from my first night here it led past a series of fire pits down to one of the smaller pools.

We stopped at a first that was unoccupied and watched the flames a moment. Like all the others, chairs and a loveseat were situated around it, and Elaine slid her hand down to mine, gently pulling me to take a seat.

The small orange coals were warm, and she turned so that her back was against my chest on the loveseat. My arm was over her shoulders, and I lifted a golden lock of her hair, sliding it back and forth.

"So what took you from military man to private eye?" She asked, watching the glow.

"I used to know the answer to that question," I said. "Now I think I'm changing my mind."

Her brow lined. "Why?"

"In the past it was about the excitement, the adventure. Then it became more about nailing bad guys and bringing them to justice."

She reached up and threaded her fingers in mine. "And now?"

I exhaled, thinking about how the past year had been, how fragmented I'd felt. "Now I haven't quite decided." I didn't want to talk about my shitty year. I wanted to know everything about her. "So did you always want to teach?"

I felt her laugh as she shook her head. "Actually, no. The truth is, I was going through a rebellious phase."

My brow lined. "What does that mean?"

"My dad wanted me to be a lawyer, just like him and my brothers, and everyone else in my family." Her tone changed, and for the first time, she was not so cheerful. "It was my way of taking control over my life."

"Sounds like you have a problem with the law." I gently poked her ribs.

She relaxed again. "I just have a problem with being ordered around."

"A sign of latent criminal tendencies." Her elbow came back sharply into my side and I grunted, "Violent criminal tendencies."

"Patrick!" she cried, and I laughed.

"No, I understand. It was your life, your future." She was still leaning against me, and my hand was on the bare skin of her upper arm. "Trust me, I've never responded well to taking orders."

"That from a guard?"

"There are different types of orders. And different sources delivering them."

"I couldn't have said it better." She sat forward and turned to me, reaching for my hands. "Let's walk some more."

I let her pull me up and we started down the path again. After a few moments, her hand moved to my arm, which I bent to hold it. "So what's so bad about being a lawyer?" I asked.

She sighed. "Nothing. It just wasn't what I wanted to do."

"You wanted to teach."

"I didn't at first, it was the only thing I knew to do. Then the more I did it, the more I loved it." She shrugged as we continued. "Every year, I had a new group of kids I fell in love with, that I watched grow and learn and become more confident. I wish some people understood that." Her tone was irritated again. "It's not about the money or the recognition, it's about making a difference. Insisting you're right all the time and bullying people won't change anything. You have to do something, be a part of the solution."

I stopped, and she stopped as well. Her green eyes met mine before she blinked down quickly. "I'm sorry."

"Don't apologize! It's impressive how much you love your work. It sounds like you're the best kind of teacher, and I'm sure whoever you're thinking about probably knows it."

She stepped forward and kissed my cheek. "Thank you," she said. "Now I want to know more about you! You have an older brother?"

"Stuart, yes," I nodded. "And he's exactly what you'd expect."

She laughed. "My older brothers all spoiled me."

"That is *not* the kind of relationship we have. If you ever encounter the big brother versus little brother stereotype, Stuart is the model for it."

Her hand was back in the crook of my arm as we walked. "But it was character-building, right?"

"No."

She laughed again, and it made me laugh, too. "See?" She cried. "You're laughing. You know I'm right."

All I knew was the sound of her voice made everything that was wrong with me feel right. The calm was back, and I felt like I could talk to her and listen to her speak and hear her thoughts all night. We walked some more, then we took a place by the fire again. She told me about her brothers and her favorite aunt—her dad's younger sister who had moved in with them after her mom left. She talked about growing up with Melissa and about living on the coast.

We sat with our bodies touching, and we sat apart, with her feet in my lap. But that never lasted long before we were back to bodies touching again. Finally, I looked around at the deserted patio and realized how late it was. I could see she was tired, and I stood, holding out my hand to help her up.

"I'll walk you back to the spa."

She nodded slowly. We didn't speak the entire way, and all I could think about were her lips and covering them with mine. I'd been thinking about it all night, but I wanted to handle this one differently — right for a change.

Stopping at the entrance, I paused, lightly cupping her cheeks. Her green eyes met mine, and she smiled. In a flash I kissed her, opening her mouth, finding her tongue for the first time. My arms moved to her waist, pulling her closer. Our bodies molded together and a little noise escaped her throat. The sound sent a blaze of desire racing through me, focusing directly below my belt. But I wasn't rushing that. Not this time.

"Goodnight." My words should have parted us, but I held her closer.

Her arms held me tightly as well, and I knew this was different from anything I'd experienced before. All of this was tectonically different.

Forcing myself to let her go, I stepped back. I couldn't look in her eyes or I'd never do what I had to do right now.

"I hope I'll see you tomorrow." An ache was in my throat.

"I'll call you." Her voice was quiet.

I turned away, and my heart, my soul, everything stayed behind as I took the first step and then the second back to the main hotel where I was staying. I'd only made it three feet when I heard her rushing up to me.

"Patrick?" It was a high whisper, and I immediately stopped, turning to face her.

She was gorgeous standing in the moonlight, the dry breeze pushing her silky hair off her shoulders. I wanted to cover those shoulders with kisses, wrap my fingers in that hair. She reached out, and I caught both her hands in mine.

"Yes?"

"I don't want you to leave me." She was breathless. "I know this is fast. It seems crazy, but... I want to spend the night in your arms."

Her delicate pink tongue touched her bottom lip, and she didn't have to ask me twice. Two steps was all it took to have her body secure against mine again. I caught her cheeks and lowered my mouth to cover her soft, beautiful lips.

Our kisses came fast, hungry, and she held my neck, my face, her hands quickly dropping to my waist, making their way under my shirt to the skin beneath. I loved her touching me. I kissed her jaw, and another noise came from her mouth. The sound killed any hesitation on my part. Breaking away, I looked around for somewhere close I could take her.

"Come with me," I said, holding her hand and leading her back the way we came. We weren't far from the smaller pool, and while it was dark and locked, I'd noticed a break in the bushes when we'd strolled past it the first time.

Leaning down, I carefully stepped through, and it took me right into the dark courtyard. Going back, Elaine was waiting and when our eyes met, she smiled. My chest rose at the sight of her, and all I could think of was sliding that dress off her body, tasting her, being inside her.

I pulled her into the small pool area and into my arms again. Our mouths collided, and I only broke contact to whip my shirt over my head. Pulling her back to me, I eased the top of her dress down, allowing her bare breasts to meet my skin, and we both sighed.

"Mmm," she breathed, moving her hands to my back and pulling me closer. The little noises coming from her with every breath had my cock straining against my zipper. I wanted to lift her against the tiled column and sink inside her right then, but I stepped back, guiding her to the cushioned lounge chair hidden in the back corner. She held the top of her dress, as if trying to pull it back up.

"No," I whispered, taking her hand away and replacing it with mine. Her breasts were heavy in my palms, and I circled my thumbs over her taut nipples. Her eyes closed and she lowered her forehead to my shoulder with a little moan. "I want these out," I said, kissing her jaw, her lips, leaning down to pull a nipple into my mouth.

Another little noise, and she kissed my neck. "What if someone sees us?"

I looked around quickly, making sure we were well hidden in the locked courtyard. "Don't worry, we're safe here."

Laying her back on the cushions, my hands slid down the smooth skin of her legs. I kissed the top of her foot, and she sighed. Traveling higher, I lifted the hem of her dress and my breath disappeared. No panties, and her skin was completely bare.

"Gorgeous," I murmured, leaning forward and kissing the inside of her thigh before sinking my tongue between her folds.

"Oh, god!" Her back arched and she cried out, clutching the sides of my head as I tasted her sweetness. I pulled her up to me, her ass in my hands, and I sucked, nipping her clit then plunging two fingers inside.

"Patrick!" she moaned as her thighs jumped. Her noises grew louder the more I kissed and sucked her.

She was sweet and swollen, a juicy peach I slid my tongue through, circling as she gasped and whimpered my name. My tongue explored every opening and crease, teasing and tasting, until I felt her coming hard against me. Her hips bucked, and I lowered her fast, condom in place. One last kiss and I plunged inside.

"Fuck me," I groaned. She was hot and tight and so slippery.

Her arms wrapped around my neck as her hips continued to rock, and I thrust again, harder. Inner muscles tensed, pulling and massaging my dick so beautifully.

"Elaine," I breathed as I kissed her shoulder, holding her body, trying to slow my pace. I didn't want it to end too fast, but I was powerless against my desire for her. My stomach clenched as need took over and my thrusting grew faster.

Her body surrounded me, tightened on me, and had me shooting over the edge. My ass tensed with each push and the sound of her moans filled my senses. Everything had gone dark, and my sole focus was the mind-blowing pleasure of my cock shooting off deep between her thighs, over and over.

"Jesus," I groaned as my orgasm slowed. My lips were on her neck and her hips moved against me. Her insides spasmed, drawing me out as she held me close, bonding me to her. I couldn't imagine letting her go.

I kissed her neck, cupping her bottom in my hands. "You are so fucking amazing," I murmured, and she started to giggle.

I leaned up to cover her mouth, smiling as I kissed her, tasting her peppermint kisses as she sighed happily and giggled again.

"Stop laughing and kiss me," I murmured against her cheek.

"Oh, god, I can't help it," she gasped, a smile in her voice. "That was fucking incredible."

I kissed her again. "Have I told you it's very sexy when you swear?"

She leaned forward to kiss me hard, quickly curling her tongue with mine before moving her lips to my ear as she whispered, "As sexy as your groans when you come inside me?"

My cock was stiffening again. "Damn, woman," I said with a grin, and she hugged me, her breasts pressing against my chest. "Keep that up, and I'll have to fuck you again."

"Mmm," she purred. "Please do."

I leaned back to remove her dress completely, but she slipped to the side. I disposed of the condom, and she took my arm.

"I want you in the pool with me." Her lips grazed mine. "Now."

I watched her skip over to the edge, quietly lowering her body as I admired her legs, her beautiful ass, her lined stomach, then her perfect breasts disappearing into the dark waters.

"Yes, ma'am," I said as she waited, submerged to her neck. I followed her, rolling a fresh condom on before lowering myself in after her.

"Mmm," she sighed as I pulled her close, her back against my chest, and slipped inside her again.

"I know it's too soon." My arms were around her waist as I kissed her ear, making my way down to her shoulder. "But I wasn't sure how I'd get it on me and into you otherwise."

She started to laugh, and I kissed her neck. One hand slid down her flat stomach between her legs, and I lightly massaged her clit. Her head dropped back on my shoulder, and she moaned softly. Leaning forwards, I scooped up her mouth, kissing her, exploring her as I held her firmly against me. I was buried in her, hard and deep, and it felt insanely good. The only way I managed to take it slow was because we'd just been this way.

The water was still heated from the day, and our bodies slid easily against each other's. Cupping her breast with my free hand, I rolled one nipple between my fingers, as another sigh escaped her lips. My hand between her legs never stopped working, gently massaging as my hips rocked slowly.

"You're so beautiful," I whispered against her ear.

Her face turned, and she said my name, a soft moan I felt all the way to my core. "I've never been like this," she whispered. "Everything in me wants you."

I moved us to where I could stand in the pool, holding her against me in the shallower water. My fingers worked her and her body heated in response. She groaned, and my legs went weak at the sound.

"I want to give you everything." I whispered before kissing her neck.

She kissed my cheek, lifting her leg and turning so that once again, we were facing each other. I couldn't hold back, and my thrusting became more rapid. Her green eyes held mine before wrinkling closed, a line piercing her forehead as she cried out a long "Ooh!"

Her thighs tightened around my waist, and everything inside her tightened. It was the most amazing sensation, a gripping from base to tip, pulling me into a frenzy. My mouth was against her temple, and I held the side of the pool as I pushed faster. Our bodies were completely entwined, waves splashing over the tiles as we moved. All sounds and motions disappeared, and I only felt her. We rocked, eyes closed and moaning, until she was pushing up against the pool wall. "Oh, god," she gasped, legs shaking hard.

She tensed and released, going from tight around me to almost pushing away, but I held her, staying with her until we finished. Until we were both spent, slowly coming down again, the quivers gradually subsiding from her limbs, calm returning.

I softly traced a line with my lips down her cheek to her jaw. She leaned her head to the side, easing my progress. "Oh my god," she sighed.

I smiled in response and kissed her. "Why aren't you with anyone?" My mouth moved to her jaw.

"I could say the same to you," she breathed. Her voice was lazy, happy.

I kissed her again, and looked at her lovely face. "Not a single man in Wilmington caught you?"

Her eyes moved away, and she shrugged. "One did."

Jealousy blazed in my stomach. Had she loved him? Did she still have feelings for him? "But you're not together anymore?"

"No," she said, hugging me close, and pressing her cheek to mine. "It's a little embarrassing."

My hands slid over the soft skin of her back as I held her, my lips touching her ear as I quietly spoke. "You don't have to be embarrassed with me." She also didn't have to tell me. But she did.

"We were together so long… I don't know why. By the end we were more like siblings than lovers." Then she turned her face away. "Why am I telling you this? How did we get on this subject?"

I moved around to kiss her lips. "I asked, and I shouldn't have. I'm sorry."

Her nose wrinkled in response. It was adorable. "I don't think you asked for that much information."

"I'm glad you trust me that much. And I'm sorry some dickhead didn't realize how sexy you are."

"I honestly thought something was wrong with me."

Catching her cheeks, I tilted her face up, covering her mouth with mine in a deep kiss. "There is nothing wrong with you," I breathed against her lips before kissing her again. "I want you in my bed."

Her arms tightened over my shoulders. "Let's go."

But in that instant, I realized. My eyes moved around the space. "We might have a problem."

Her green eyes rolled. "No towels!"

"Hang on." I slid out and away, going to the side and pushing my body out of the water. I picked up the thin white undershirt I'd worn beneath my pinstriped oxford and held it up. "It probably won't help much, but you can use this to dry off.

She was beside me in an instant, taking it and rubbing it over her wet body. The sight of that almost did me in.

"That'll do," she whispered. "I mean, my dress is strapless anyway."

I watched as she stepped in and pulled it over her bare breasts until I couldn't resist. I scooped her up against me. "You are so damned sexy."

"Patrick!" she shrieked a laugh. "Why did I even dry off?"

Releasing her quickly, I stepped back. "Sorry."

But she threw her arms around my neck, hugging against me again.

"Don't ever stop doing that." Her lips brushed mine. "Ever."

My arms were back around her in an instant. "I promise I won't."

## CHAPTER 9:
## BEST DAY EVER

Dawn pierced through the crack I'd tried not to leave in the curtains, but I didn't mind. With the growing light, I was able to see her better as she slept next to me, her arm loosely across my waist, her silky blonde hair streaming over my pillow. I had to force myself to keep still and not slide my hand down the smooth skin of her back.

Last night, I'd made love to her every way I could before we were both falling asleep, still holding each other. Something was happening here — not alcohol, not escape. Being with Elaine Was like... nothing I'd ever had. I wanted to tell her I could fall in love with her as I watched her eyes drift closed and her breathing soften, but it was way too soon. And I had all that shit to deal with back home.

Still, nothing had prepared me for Elaine. Nothing in my past had this intensity. No relationship, no job, nothing had ever felt the way I did when we talked, when we touched, when her body wrapped around mine. For the first time in a year, I could honestly say what happened with Stacy was for the best. It truly felt like everything had conspired to draw me to this place specifically to meet this woman.

She stirred and rolled onto her side, her green eyes blinking open slowly. When she saw me, she smiled, and my heart warmed.

"Patrick," she said, moving her cheek to my chest, her soft blonde hair spilling over my arm. I smoothed it back. "Did you get enough sleep?"

I didn't say I couldn't be bothered with sleep with her in my bed. All I wanted was to make her happy. "Yes," I answered.

She made a contented sound before rolling onto her back to stretch. I was right beside her, kissing her stomach that flattened as her back arched, working my way higher. Instantly she curled together with a laugh.

I pulled her to me. "What do you think about touring Scottsdale with me?"

Her arms snaked around my waist. "I thought you had to be in meetings all morning."

"Fuck meetings, I'm spending my time with you."

I felt her laugh more. "Then yes, I would love to tour Scottsdale with you!"

Standing, I took her hand. "Let me walk you back so we can get changed. If this is your first visit, there are some places you've got to see." I had the whole day planned out already.

* * *

Derek didn't hassle me about skipping the day's meetings, which was surprising. "You've landed some good clients on this trip," he said, and his voice was so changed, I almost didn't recognize it. "I'm taking the afternoon off as well."

"Okay." What was going on with him? Then I remembered to ask, "Did you find Melissa? Elaine tried to call her at one point, but she didn't answer."

"Hm," was all he said.

My brows pulled together. "Last night? Melissa? You went after her?"

"Right." He cleared his throat, and I could swear it sounded like he was smiling. "I mean, yes, we had dinner. She's... well. I mean, she's just fine."

If I was meeting anyone besides Elaine, I would've stayed until I got answers, but I *was* meeting Elaine. "Well, see you tonight," I said. "And when we get back, you're going to tell me what the hell's going on."

"Have fun," he said, that smile still in his voice.

I hung up wondering if he'd ever told me to have fun before. Previously, I'd been convinced he didn't know the meaning of the phrase. I decided to let it go. Grabbing the keys to my rental and my phone, I hustled down to the lobby.

* * *

Scottsdale with Elaine by my side seemed brighter and more interesting than it ever had before. I took her to the Frank Lloyd Wright estate, and she took pictures of the unusual statues and plants growing on the land along with the house built into the landscape. Then I took her to Camelback Mountain to climb the assorted flights of stairs that seemed to go straight up to the sky embedded throughout the red-rock hillsides.

In the cleft of one of the boulders, I took her hand and pulled her onto my lap. We were sitting on a low cliff, and the 360 degree view of the city below was breathtaking. She exhaled and leaned her head back against my shoulder.

"How do you know about all this?" she asked as I laced our fingers together. "Did you live here before?"

"One of my uncles owned a winter home here," I said, kissing her neck. "We came a few times to visit when I was in high school."

"It's so different from anywhere else. Barren and rocky, but still green and colorful."

"Mm-hm," I said, running my lips behind her ear as my hands searched for her skin beneath the front of her shirt. "And hot," I added.

She turned her lips to my cheek as my fingers lightly touched her stomach, traveling higher until I found the edge of her bra. Her sigh whispered across my skin as I pushed the garment aside. I loved her breasts, soft in my hands and slightly heavy. I pinched her tight nipples and a little noise came from her throat. Her head was on my shoulder, eyes closed, and her breath was growing faster as I massaged her. I wanted to replace my hands with my mouth. Just the thought was causing some pretty significant heat to rise in my pants.

"I have never enjoyed this city so much," I said against her neck, and she laughed.

Just then a head popped up at our feet. "Oh," a male voice said loudly.

Elaine squealed and jumped off my lap, turning her back as the hiker apologized and attempted to climb back down.

"Sorry," I said, clearing my throat as I tried discreetly to adjust my fly.

Elaine caught my hand and jerked me with her away from the edge and to the steps leading down the mountain. I laughed as I followed her. "Slow down, you'll trip. And it's impossible to run with a hard-on."

Instantly, she turned back into my arms, burying her head in my shoulder. I caught her, hugging her close as she straightened her bra laughing. "We have to go. I'll die if I see that person again."

I grinned as I held her, and once her underthings were back in place, she turned and began walking again. "I'm sorry," I said, catching her hand. "You're just so damned sexy."

"Where are we headed next?"

"Back to my room?"

Stopping, she wrapped her arms around my neck and kissed my nose. "You are supposed to be showing me Scottsdale." Those green eyes pierced right into mine, and I was gone. Anything she wanted.

I kissed her lips briefly before catching her hand and taking the lead again. "There's a ghost town south of here. They do tours and Old West shows. You'll love it."

We spent the rest of the day in the shadow of the Superstition Mountains exploring mines, looking at antique photographs, and wandering through souvenir shops. I bought her a sterling silver ring embossed with a turquoise Kokopelli, and after several hours, we headed back to the resort dusty, tired, and hungry.

Again, when I helped her out of the car at the entrance to the spa, I could barely let her go, but we were meeting up again for dinner in a few short hours. "Tell Melissa you're spending the night with me," I said, catching her cheeks and kissing her.

She nodded, holding out her hand. "I love my ring. I don't think I'll ever take it off." Then she wrapped her arms around my neck. "It's silly, but this felt like the best day ever."

"Even when the hiker caught me feeling you up?"

She laughed and pinched my arm. "You're such a guy."

"I lo—" *Shit.* I stopped myself. "I'll see you tonight."

Her expression changed, as if she knew what I'd almost said. She blinked down a moment, seeming lost in thought. Then she smiled and gave me a quick kiss before dashing into the resort. I leaned back against the car thinking about all of it.

## CHAPTER 10:
## BACK TO REALITY

As if some cosmic hand had pushed the advance button on the remainder of our trip, the time flew. We'd had a dinner with Melissa and Derek in which they stayed at the table with us the entire time, but I honestly couldn't remember much of what was said or what happened. All I saw was Elaine.

We'd gone straight back to my room, barely making it through the door before clothes started flying and we were in the bed, mouths searching for every uncovered piece of skin they could find.

The last day we'd spent in Sedona, stopping along the way at roadside vendors and hiking trails that were all irritatingly well-populated. Our final night we spent in my room, ordering desserts and wine from room service, making love, and talking over the television show we weren't watching.

"What will you do when you get back," I asked, twisting a strand of golden hair around my finger as she lay with her cheek against my bare chest.

"Back to school," she said, lifting up and reaching for the glass of wine on the bedside table. As she sipped, I noticed her eyes traveling up my stomach then meeting mine. It was pretty hot, and when she saw I'd busted her, she laughed. "You have great genes."

I glanced to the chair, going for a tease. "They were actually my brother's, but they didn't fit him."

She snorted a laugh, and covered her face with her hand.

"What?" I smiled.

"I was talking about your body." Without hesitation, she reached forward and ran a finger down my stomach, tracing every line. "You're totally ripped. How often do you work out?"

Catching her hand, I pulled it to my lips. "Couple times a week. Derek needed a spotter, and I didn't have anything better to do." All this touching and kissing was getting me going again. "Besides, you're pretty toned yourself." I'd noticed the lines on her torso.

"Pilates," she said, reaching across me again to put her glass back on the table. With her naked, body stretched over mine, I couldn't help running my finger down the line of her back. Her stomach bent as she set the glass down, and she rose up, pushing me back against the pillows with all her weight. It wasn't much, but I let her win.

"That tickles," she laughed.

"Have I mentioned I love how physical you are?"

"Funny you should say that." In an instant she was up, pulling my arm. I followed her out of bed, wondering at the mischievous glint in her eye. "I was thinking…"

A few seconds ticked by, and I finally asked, "What?"

She took my hand, pulling me and then turning me by my arms until I was sitting in the desk chair. Her maneuvering me around completely naked had my dick as aroused as my curiosity.

"Are you going to tell me what's going on?" I asked.

Going behind me, she held my hands together at the base of the chair. Her hair tickled my biceps as she leaned into my ear, and I felt her bare breast graze my shoulder. "Do you ever have to arrest anyone, Mr. Knight?"

A smile curled the side of my mouth. I could get into a little role-play. "I'm not a cop, Ms. Merritt. I don't have handcuffs."

"That's too bad," she said softly, reaching for something I didn't see. I was seriously getting turned on until I felt her tying my wrists together.

"Is that my good tie?" I tried to pull away, but she'd made a solid knot. "Elaine," I said as she circled back around, trailing her finger across my shoulder before straddling my waist, facing me.

Her breasts grazed my chest, and a mixture of arousal and irritation stirred below my waist.

"Can you get loose?" she whispered in my ear. "Or are you my captive?"

"Untie me," I growled, but she only kissed my neck, slipping her hand down to my rigid cock.

*Fuck.* I was pissed at being tied, but damn if I didn't have a major hard-on. Her lips feathered a kiss against my ear, and I jerked against the knot.

"I think you like it." She was at my ear again, moving her hand up and down my shaft. My eyes closed as I suppressed a groan. What she was doing felt amazing, and I wanted to touch her. I wanted my fucking hands untied. Pleasure tingled through my groin as my stomach tightened.

"Fuck." Anger mixed with lust mixed with something weirdly primal twisted inside me, and I jerked against the knot again. "When I get loose—"

"What?" She caught my chin with her free hand, holding my cheeks and forcing me to look into her eyes. It pissed me off, but she was grinning. I fucking loved it. "You're going to fuck me?"

My chest tightened, and I snapped my face away. Desire-laced frustration was building in my torso. "I'm going to fuck you hard."

"Mmm." Both her hands held my face now. "You get a kiss for that."

Leaning forward, she lightly touched her lips to mine, pulling away when I tried to kiss her back. Again, my muscles strained, and I jerked harder against the knot. Her kiss turned rough. She pushed me back, opening my mouth with hers, pushing her tongue inside. Everything in me tightened. I was about to come. I was going crazy, and all I could think about was getting my hands loose and getting them on her.

Her hand returned to the tip of my cock, and I could feel it slippery now. With my eyes closed, my were senses focused on the depth of her kiss, her hand on my dick, and the gradual loosening of that tie. Tightness burst in my stomach as my first arm slipped free.

She noticed it move, and with a shriek, she was off my lap, headed for the bed. But I caught her, pulling her back and slamming into her from behind as we fell together onto the mattress. I held her hips and fucked her hard, and somewhere in the cloud of my angry-frustrated-turned-on-as-hell brain, I heard her cries. It was sick and twisted, and damn. My brain had switched over to primal, and all I knew was her depth, her tightness and that urge to dominate driving me as I gripped her ass, hitting it harder.

"Oh, god, Patrick," she moaned. Somehow she managed to get her knees under her, and she pushed back. We moved up with her on my lap, arching her back against my chest, deepening my penetration.

"Fuck!" I was going off deep inside her, holding her breasts as she rode me, lifting and dropping as I sat on my knees behind her.

Hot, wet, power, need, more—all the feelings twisted together as I finished. My mixture of emotions made it difficult to know where we were, if she'd made it or not. I was momentarily blinded. We fell forward again on the bed, still connected, and I held her as she finished rocking against me. I massaged her clit and kissed her shoulders, the space behind her neck, up to her ears. She continued moaning and moving against me until slowly, we came down, breathing heavily.

I was spent, rolling onto my back beside her. All the adrenaline that had been raging inside me was now satisfaction mixed with relief. "What the fuck was that about?" My voice was ragged.

Still lying on her stomach, she turned her head, sneaking a peek at me. "It seemed to be about you dominating."

"I hope you're on the pill." I bent my elbows, pushing my fingers into the sides of my hair. Protection had not crossed my mind. I had only thought about one thing just then and we'd done it. She reached up and pulled my elbow nearest her down, watching my face.

"I am." Her voice was soft, and I looked over at her.

"You probably ruined my best tie."

"I'm sorry."

I was calmer now, and the guilty smile on her face was bringing me around. "You're taking a big risk tying a guy up like that. You're lucky I don't have any kind of PTSD."

"I was just playing with you. Are you mad?"

Hell no, I thought. I wasn't sure what I felt. "Where did you learn to make knots like that?"

That grin was still pulling on the corner of her mouth. "I told you, I have older brothers."

I rose up on my elbow then, looking down at her. "If you pull a stunt like that again, I'll wear you out. I do *not* like being tied up."

Shyness gone, she laughed. "You don't have to tell me, I was here. It was intense."

Her finger touched my nose, running down to my lips. I kissed it and caught her waist, pulling her body to me. "Don't do it again."

"You liked it."

"I'm stronger than you, and I could hurt you."

"Sounds like we need a safe word."

My head dropped to her shoulder, and I felt her laugh again, which made me laugh. She was wild, but in a way that surprised and amazed me. Raising my head, I caught her mouth, giving her a rough kiss. "I've got my eye on you."

Her arms wrapped around my neck. "I want your eyes on me." She kissed my lips lightly. "I want your thoughts on me. Only me. All the time."

She had no idea. I kissed her again, and she kissed me back. Strong and good and full of feelings neither of us would say out loud yet. But we were getting there. I lowered my face to her chest and wrapped my arms around her waist. The sound of her breath swirling in and out filled my ear and holding her body next to mine, I couldn't help but wonder, how in the hell would I let her go tomorrow? I had no fucking idea.

\* \* \*

I'd completely forgotten to close the damn curtains when we finally fell asleep last night, and now I was regretting it as the desert sun poured in full-force. At some point, I'd woken up and she was still in my arms. I'd kissed her head and fallen asleep again with her warm body secure against mine, but this time, when I reached out, she was gone.

The shower was going, and I was about to join her when the water shut off, and I heard her moving quickly. I hated the thought of what was coming — this separation was going to hurt like hell. I wasn't even sure how far Wilmington was from Princeton, but I was pretty confident it was more than a few hours. Still, we could figure it out. I was willing to try, anyway.

The door opened and she paused a moment when she saw me awake. Her blonde hair was damp and had the slightest wave, and a towel was tied under her arms. God, she was so fucking gorgeous. A small smile, a swift kiss to my cheek, and she scooped up the dress she'd been wearing last night. She was back in the bathroom before I could catch her.

"I've got to go," she said as she returned fully clothed. "I haven't packed or anything."

"Hang on." I stepped into the bathroom to take care of both my issues. One of which, I'd much rather have taken care of with her. "Give me a second to change, and I'll walk you back."

My shoulders were tight, my whole body was tight as I walked back and sat on the bed, picking up my shorts. This moment had felt far away last night, and now it was playing out way too fast.

"No time!" She kissed my cheek. Her long blonde hair slipped forward into my face, but I caught her as she tried to pull away.

"Elaine. Slow down," I said with more force. "It won't take me two seconds to pull on my jeans and a shirt."

"Patrick." Her tone stopped me. "I want to say goodbye here."

Studying her expression, I wasn't sure how to respond. "That sounds very final."

She exhaled and sat beside me on the bed not meeting my eyes. "I was awake most of the night thinking, and... I just can't take another long goodbye."

"So we won't say it. Let's make a plan."

Her head shook out a no. "You've got your job, I've got my job. The school year's just starting... We're almost a day apart in distance. It's only a matter of time before—"

"Before nothing. We can make it work."

Her green eyes met mine then. "How?"

My eyebrows rose. "Do we have to know right this second?"

Taking my hand, she pulled it onto her lap. Then she ran her fingertip along the tattoo that no longer said *Stacy*. "These last few days have been amazing. You're gorgeous and funny and sexy..." She took a deep breath and met my eyes then. "And I can't do long-distance,

Patrick. I just can't. It's too hard, and it always ends badly."

The ache in my stomach was growing stronger. I hadn't expected her to be like this. Not after last night. "You're so certain."

"Can't we just keep what we shared these last few days as a beautiful memory? Instead of trying to hold on and ruining it all?"

I was feeling pretty ruined already. "Why are you doing this?"

"Please, Patrick," her voice was a whisper now. "Don't make this harder than it is."

Fuck that. "Is this hard for you? Because you're making it look pretty damn easy."

She stood fast and grabbed her bag, but I was right with her, catching her arm.

"Wait." Yes, I was pissed. I couldn't believe she was doing this. I didn't understand why she was doing it after all we'd shared. But I didn't want those to be my last words. I didn't want to have any last words, but fuck if we left it that way.

She wouldn't look at me as I took her phone from her hand, typing in my number. It was a shot in the dark, and I was taking it. Quickly, I hit save and handed it back to her, my voice gentler.

"That's my number. For when you change your mind. Call me, and I'll be there."

For a moment she only held the device. Then without a word or even a look back she turned and pushed through the door. Everything in me wanted to catch her, to hold her, to bring her back and make her say she didn't want this, but she was gone. The room was dead quiet in her absence. The only reminder she'd been here was the fresh smell of the spa-issued shampoo she used.

Slowly, like a drop of dye in a glass of water, the pain hit my chest. It threaded its way down my shredded insides to my aching stomach, spreading out in my abdomen. I sat again briefly then I lay back on the bed, staring at the ceiling.

With five words, she'd walked out the door. She didn't do long distance. I didn't know what the hell to do with that. Or even what to say. And fuck all of it, I'd been down that road, holding onto a woman who had other plans. I'd be damned if I did it again.

It was just... Elaine was different from anything I'd had before. We had something worth holding onto, worth trying to keep.

But I couldn't force her to see it. All I could do was let her go and wait. See if she realized it and called me. *Dammit.* Blinking, I cleared my throat, and stood, shaking it off and quickly going to the bathroom to hit the shower.

Cleaned and dressed, I roughly threw all my shit in my suitcase. Derek and I had different flights back to Princeton. His departed later than mine, so I didn't have to see him before I left the resort. I called to let him know I was heading out, but I got voicemail.

"It's me." The change in my voice was apparent, defeated. "Heading out. See you back at the office."

Back to reality.

I tried to stoke that confidence—she would come around. But how could I know that? We'd only been together a few days. Picking up my suitcase, I walked out of the room, and the dry, twisting ache of what I was leaving behind went with me.

# CHAPTER 11:
## WHATEVER IT TAKES

Instead of going in, I left a message that I was sick. Partly because the last thing I felt like doing was dealing with Star, but mostly because I couldn't get out of bed. Lying on my side, I couldn't stop thinking about Elaine.

I tried to reason with myself. It didn't make sense for me to be so torn up inside. I'd had other women. Hell, I'd loved one woman enough to ask her to marry me. But I'd never felt consumed by the mere thought of touching someone before. Everything in me was drawn to Elaine. She said she wanted to be the only one I thought about, and she'd gotten her wish. And it fucking hurt like hell.

Rolling onto my side, I kicked my ass out of bed. I wasn't doing this. Yes, she was gorgeous and sexy and amazing. And she ended it. She didn't want a long-distance relationship, and whatever had happened between us wasn't enough to change that. It didn't make sense, but I had to deal with it. If she never came back, I would work through the pain twisting a hole in the center of my gut and get over it.

Food tasted like cardboard. I tried unpacking, but the second shirt I pulled out that smelled like Cactus Flower perfume almost had me throwing things. If I tried to sleep, all I saw were her eyes, her body, her smile. Walking around my apartment, I knew I couldn't spend the day here like this. Sick or not, I got dressed and went to work. Anything was better than being here alone thinking about her.

* * *

I walked through the glass doors that read Alexander-Knight, LLC, and for a moment surprise pushed out all my other emotions. Nikki was there behind the front desk.

"You're back?" I said. "But what about..."

A big smile covered her face, and she hopped up, circling the desk to hug me. As always, she wore a tight wrap-dress showing off her sex-kitten figure. I think the dress was peach-colored, but her appearance didn't interest me as much today. She pressed her body against mine in a hug, and I bent my elbows to return her embrace. Still I was confused. *Where was Star?*

"How are you, handsome?" She stepped back, evaluating my expression. "Hmm... not so good either. Derek's acting like his favorite pet got run over. He's been in his office with the door closed all morning."

"I don't think he has any pets," I said absently.

Nikki breathed a short laugh. "What happened to my guys in the two weeks I was gone? Did you miss me that much?"

My hand automatically went to my stomach, covering the spot where the pain was most intense. "Jet-lag. You know how it is traveling across country."

"Actually, I don't, but I do know what jet-lag looks like, and it ain't this."

Discussing my heartache with Nikki or anyone else was not about to happen. "Well, I'm glad you're back." I forced a smile and headed to my office.

Flipping through my case, I pulled out the cards and information from the clients I'd met and tried to care about them. Derek gave me a portfolio describing the different levels of service we offered, from Level One, which was strictly enforcement—an online network got hacked, we tracked down the hackers—all the way up to designing the network and integrating it into our system for round the clock monitoring and troubleshooting.

He'd also returned from Dallas with that huge corporate-phishing ring we were supposed to track down. All of it combined to being more than enough work to bury myself in for as long as it took to stop feeling it. To stop needing her.

I went to the server and pulled up our standard business letter for new clients and started typing up the first proposal.

* * *

Calm put in an appearance around two o'clock. I'd worked solid through lunch, sent out the welcome packages to my new clients then spent several hours analyzing the email accounts from the phishing ring. A pattern was forming, but whether it matched the same scam being used across servers was as yet unclear. My mind was effectively numbed by the repetition of tracking URLs and looking up owners in the *whois* database, and I needed to walk around.

I went down the hall toward Derek's office. As far as I knew, his door had been closed all day, but I knocked. He'd been distracted the whole time we were in Scottsdale, so I wasn't bothered by his strange behavior now. What did bother me was that since we'd returned, he seemed sadly distracted instead of happily.

"How's it going," he said, focused on his computer.

"It's coming together. I'm starting to see a pattern."

"Good," he nodded.

"So what's up with the Star situation?" I sat in the same square leather chair I'd occupied my first day here when he'd read my resume for ten minutes, royally pissing me off.

He looked up from his laptop then made a few quick clicks before leaning back. "You're not looking so great today."

"You look pretty shitty yourself, but enough about us. Why's Nikki back?"

He looked down at his desk a moment before speaking. "The other girl took a different job. And I asked if Nikki could come back."

That pulled me forward—I was almost relieved. "The other girl? You mean Star?"

Derek's brow pierced, and his blue eyes cut to mine. "Remember when you suspected a setup?"

"Yeah?"

"It's possible your instincts were right."

"What the hell?" He paused, thinking, while I waited impatiently for the rest. "What happened?"

He exhaled, picking up a pen. "I finally caught up with my aunt, and she was confused by everything I told her. She said the temp had called in and said she

126

wouldn't be able to start with us until Monday. Sick kid or something. Then she said she took another job."

"But—"

"Right. But Star showed up on Thursday."

"And she never mentioned having a kid."

"Or a husband."

My lips pressed together, and I leaned back in the chair again. "Good point. So what makes you think it's a setup?"

"The other girl's name was Monica."

"The fuck!" I was out of the chair then and pacing. "So what now?"

Derek shrugged. "Nothing. We don't have anything to go on. Stuart and I never felt the need to install security cameras in the office, so we have no images." He paused, slanting an eye at me. "And God knows I don't need to see whatever you're doing behind closed doors."

I let it pass. "But the building has cameras. The elevators?"

He shook his head. "Already checked. She kept her head down the whole way in and out."

"So she fucking wouldn't get caught." I couldn't believe I'd been set up. But why?

"Which means we don't have an image to run through the databases."

"I could probably describe her well enough to a sketch artist."

Derek stood and joined me by the windows looking out at the courtyard below. "At this point, I say leave it. Nobody's asked for anything or made any demands. If anything comes of it, then we'll do something."

The anger burning my insides was compounded by the frustration I was already feeling. "That's not good enough. I want to know who and why."

"I understand that." For a moment we didn't speak. "Is there anybody you know of who might be after you?" he asked.

I shook my head. "I mean, sure there are people I've sent up, but nothing that would warrant something like this. I don't even know what she was after. She never asked for anything."

"And you stuck your dick in it." He exhaled and went back to his chair, taking a seat and reopening his laptop. "Nope. I say we leave well enough alone."

My lips tightened. There was no fucking way I was letting this go. I'd gotten too close, and I'd be damned if I didn't find out what this was about. If he was out, I would do it on my own.

"So what's up with that other thing?" I asked before I left.

His eyes moved from the laptop to me. "What other thing?"

"Whatever had you so distracted in the desert."

He stared back at his computer, made a few clicks, then leaned back in his chair, steepling his fingers.

"Hey, you said it was my fault. I should know what I did." I hoped a joke might loosen him up some. I was not expecting it to work.

"I met someone. The first night we were there." He leaned forward on the desk, picking up his pen again. "I'm in love with her. But it's complicated."

"Met someone? I only ever saw you with..." Realization washed over me. "It's Melissa?"

He didn't answer—he didn't have to. The answer was clear on his face.

Having my own heart freshly ripped out had me feeling generous. "Want to grab a beer after work?"

He looked up at me. "That actually sounds good."

"Just head to my office when you're ready." I was at the door when I paused. "And I'm glad you got Nikki back."

"She knows the office," he said quietly. "I'm not traveling anytime soon, and at least I know what to watch out for."

Pointing out he might try discussing the problem with her didn't feel like the right thing to say at the moment. Besides I could probably help with that—later. For now, I had another matter to investigate.

\* \* \*

Derek was on his fourth beer, and I was two vodkas in. We'd hit the time of the evening when we started wondering aloud why we didn't do this more often, and it was all brotherhood and bonding.

"She was not what I expected to find," he said. "And then, it was like I was powerless against her."

"I know that feeling," I said, holding my glass aloft.

His hand went to his eyes, which he rubbed too hard. "I can't stop thinking about her."

"I know that fucking feeling, too." I finished the vodka in one long drink. Then I signaled the bartender for another. Looked like I'd be taking a cab home tonight. "How did you figure this was my fault again?"

He lowered his hand and laughed bitterly. "All your acting up and talk about living. I'm sure you put the idea in my head."

"You're welcome," I said, watching the bartender prep my next drink. It was back in front of me again, and I stared down at the contents.

"Now all I do is wonder what she's doing," he paused. "I wonder if the way I felt was all just me. If she's with him now."

His last words were so quiet, they were almost inaudible. I watched his grip tighten on the glass, and that knot twisted in my own throat as I admitted the truth in my head. My thoughts were running in the exact same circles.

Elaine had said she'd just broken up with someone, and all I could wonder was if she'd gone back to him. If the jackass had woken up and realized how amazing she was. If he wanted her back. Would she go back to him? Would she forget me that easily?

My fist went down hard against the bar, and I picked up the drink, almost draining the glass in one long gulp.

"You and Elaine got pretty close," he said, glancing at me. "Are you still talking to her?"

"No," I said through the thickness in my voice. "We haven't talked since we've been back."

Memories of holding her body to me, of kissing her slowly tormented me. Flashes of her lips against mine, her breasts on my chest, her tying me up... I growled, sitting back and shoving my fingers against my forehead.

"I can't do this." I was off the stool and pulling on my jacket. "I've got to go."

I fished for my wallet, but Derek stopped me. "I'll cover it," he said.

"Sure?"

"Yeah. Sorry if I hit a sore spot. Again."

"Don't worry about it."

With a fist bump to the shoulder, I left him sitting at the bar. I had to get out of there. I didn't want to think about Elaine, but nothing would stop my brain from drowning in her memory. In the past, alcohol had been a guaranteed solution to the bad feelings. Alcohol or sex. But I couldn't drink her away tonight, and the thought of touching another woman turned my stomach. I only wanted her. I wanted her so bad it hurt.

*Bee stings... needles... rope burns...* Hailing a cab, I passed my hand over my face again. *Jesus, this fucking ache.* I had to fucking get back to the office and get to the bottom of the Star setup. And I was going to break the phishing ring, and I was going to work out, and sleep, and eat my meals, and put one damned foot in front of the other, and do whatever the fuck it took to make this time pass. Until I didn't think about her any more. Until it didn't hurt.

I was going to need a lot more work.

## Chapter 12:
### Something Bigger

Trying to find Star without a photo ID was like trying to find a needle in a haystack. I'd started with the database of prostitution arrests in the last five years. She was too good not to be a professional, but I wasn't convinced she'd have a record. Still, it was the only idea my instincts suggested, so I followed it.

My eyes were crossing looking at photo after photo of bleached-blonde mugshots when I noticed I wasn't alone. Pausing from my nonstop scrolling, I looked up to see Nikki standing in my doorway, hip cocked, eyebrow arched.

"I was beginning to wonder what was going to make you look up." Her rose-lined pink lips curled into a smile, and the tightness in my chest eased slightly.

"What's up?" I asked. Derek and I might have come back to the office changed, but Nikki was the same as always. Teased hair, huge earrings, tight dresses. Funny how her efforts didn't capture my attention so much anymore.

"I thought you might take me to lunch. Unless you're skipping it again today?"

"Have I been skipping lunch?" My brow lined as I looked toward the clock. Already two.

"Come on," she said, stepping around my desk and catching my arm. "I'll let you buy me a salad in the cafeteria."

"There's a cafeteria?"

"In Building C."

"I'm glad I've got you and Derek around. Otherwise, I might miss all the hidden perks of this complex."

She exhaled a laugh. "The food isn't that great, but they make a decent salad. And I think Derek said the bacon club isn't bad."

Outside, I noticed the season was starting to change. Soon the holidays would begin, but I was glad they were a ways off. I wasn't in the mood. We walked quietly through the courtyard and entered the third building to our left. My thoughts were preoccupied with the search for Star and how I wasn't finding a damn thing. She could be anywhere. Hell, for all I knew, she was from another city, another state altogether. Derek was probably right. I should just forget it. Count myself lucky and wait to see if anything ever even came of it.

That just didn't sit right with me.

"Jesus," Nikki broke through my distraction. "I've never seen two men more changed. What the hell happened while I was gone?"

My eyebrows rose as I took in her posture, leaned back in the chair, she had both hands on her hips as she studied me. Her salad appeared untouched.

"Sorry, Nik," I said, picking up the club sandwich I'd ordered. "You'd be surprised all the shit that went down after you left."

"I'll take that as your funny way of saying you missed me."

In spite of myself I laughed. "I was pissed at Derek when you left." I took a bite. "But that was just the beginning."

She leaned forward and poked her salad with her fork, not eating. After a few quiet moments, she shook her head. "Are you going to tell me?"

Dropping the sandwich, I grabbed a paper napkin and wiped my hands roughly. "First, you can't tell Derek," I exhaled. "He told me to drop it."

A smile curled the side of her mouth. "You're worried about me ratting you out to *Derek*?"

"Yeah, well, I've fucked up enough on this one." I shook my head, throwing the paper on the table.

"Go on."

"Derek called the temp agency after you left, and a woman came." I felt like such a fool saying it out loud to her. "I thought she was your replacement, and I gave her access to everything."

Nikki's brow creased, and she leaned forward. "What happened?"

Clearing my throat, I leaned back. "I kind of... Well, I kind of slept with her."

"What!?"

"In the office," I hastened along. "And it turns out, she wasn't your replacement. We don't know who she was."

Shaking her head, Nikki spoke. "Are you saying a woman who you thought was my replacement came to the office and you slept with her?" Her eyes blinked rapidly. "How long was she there before that happened?"

"Look, I fucked up, okay? I know it. We were drinking, and the next thing I knew, she was on my dick."

Her face morphed into an expression of disapproval, which irritated me, but her words cancelled it all out.

"Everybody makes mistakes. Learn from it and move on." She finally started eating. "What happened next?"

"That's just it. Derek sent me to Scottsdale, and she disappeared. We got back, and his aunt told him *Monica* took another job."

"Monica was the one you slept with?" She forked more lettuce.

"No," I said, picking up a chip. "The person I met was named Star."

Ducking toward her plate, Nikki pulled her paper napkin up quickly to cover her mouth. "Oh my god, her name was *Star*?" Giggles. "And you, an experienced detective fell for that?"

I was ready to go. "Look, I'm not in the mood. I'm trying to find out what the hell happened and fix it. Or at least get answers."

"I'm sorry." She shook her head and reached out to cover my hand with hers. "Seriously, I'll stop teasing you."

I took a sip of the cold drink I'd ordered, feeling less like talking than ever.

"I'm sure Derek was pissed," she continued, "but I have to say, the way you two have been acting, I would think it was something bigger than a rogue temp who turned out to be... what? A spy?"

I shrugged. "I don't know what she wanted. That's why I've been working so hard. I need to know."

Her lips poked out and she nodded. Then she picked up her drink and took a long pull from the straw. "And that's it? There's nothing else?"

Images of Elaine's smile, her shiny blonde hair, her green eyes trickled across my memory in a cool stream. I blinked hard. "Pretty much," I said quietly.

"You sure?" Nikki leaned forward on the table, allowing the top of her dress to dip forward. From this angle, I had the full view of her awesome cleavage, but it didn't matter. All I wanted was Elaine.

"Yeah." I lifted my drink and took another sip.

She sat back in her chair. "Wow. You're seriously hung up. Is it on this Star person? Is that why you're so obsessed with finding her?"

"What?" my voice rose. "No way. Elaine's nothing like that psycho."

Her smile returned as her voice softened. "So tell me about Elaine."

My eyes closed briefly, but it was pointless trying to resist. "She's beautiful. I…" I couldn't say that. "I want to be with her, but she lives in Wilmington, and long distance isn't her thing." I picked up the silverware knife and rolled it in my fingers.

"But you'd do anything to see her again." Nikki's voice was gentle, and my gaze blinked to hers. The warmth in her eyes was almost unbearable.

"Anything."

She leaned forward then, but this time when her hand covered mine, there was no confrontation, no teasing. Her voice was serious. "Patrick," she said quietly. "You're in love."

Jerking my hand back, I put the knife back on the table and stood. "It was less than a week. And now it's over." Pain radiated through my chest, but I kept it together. "Now I just want to find out who the fuck is messing with me and why."

I started to go, but then I remembered and stepped back, fishing in my pocket for my cash. Nikki's lips were pursed as she watched me toss a couple twenties on the table. She didn't say anything, but I had a pretty good idea what she was thinking—like it mattered.

"See you back at the office."

The wind outside had picked up, and damp air hit me straight in the face. It looked like a storm was rolling in, but I didn't mind. I actually hoped it would rain. Lately, I'd sought out all sorts of unpleasant feelings, anything to match or block out the raging noise in my chest. A storm felt exactly right at this moment.

\* \* \*

Two more days of studying URLs and the *whois* database compiling locations for the phishing scam went by. Two more days of scrolling through endless mugshots from all over the New Jersey area trying to find that face went by. Time was passing, but nothing inside me was changing. I searched for Star obsessively, but mugshot after mugshot was blurring my memory of her. It wasn't like I'd gotten a long look at her before we started drinking anyway, and I was losing my motivation to find her. I was losing my motivation to do anything. Elaine's face was all I could see.

By Friday afternoon, I was sitting behind my desk feeling like I was going crazy when my phone rang. I picked it up without even looking at the face. "Hello?" I heard my tone—impatient, tense, frustrated. Then I heard the voice that took my breath away.

"Patrick?" Her voice was high, and it sounded slightly nervous.

Every muscle down to my core tightened at the sound. "Elaine?" I wasn't sure what to say next. She'd called me. "How are you?"

Her throat cleared, and my eyes closed. I could see her perfectly in my mind.

"I, um..." Her voice became quiet. "I..." A sound like something covering the phone filled my ear. I couldn't make out what was happening.

"Elaine?" I repeated, my whole body tense. "Is everything okay?"

A sharp sniff and my chest clutched. Was she crying?

"I'm sorry," she said, clearing her throat again, but I heard the smallest tremor as she spoke. That's when I knew she was struggling for control.

Another sniffle, and I couldn't take it anymore. "What's wrong, baby?" My voice was now gentle.

"Oh, Patrick." At that she completely broke down. "I miss you so much."

Emotion flooded my limbs, making me temporarily weak. In an instant, I was on my feet, grabbing my keys and wallet. "I'll be there in six hours."

"No," she sniffed, her voice tenuous. "I can't let you do that."

I was unable to stop the smile crossing my face. "You couldn't stop me if you tried."

"Oh, god," she breathed. "Patrick..." From her tone, I could see her beautiful eyes close, the smile on her lips. "It'll take longer than six hours. I checked."

"I'm walking out the door now," I said, giving Nikki a brief wave as I pushed through the main glass entrance. "I'm not stopping until you're in my arms."

A little laugh met my ears, and my heart felt like it flew out of my chest to where she was. "Please be safe," she whispered.

"Don't worry."

## CHAPTER 13:
## REUNITED THIS WAY

Elaine was in my arms, her hands in my hair, her legs around my waist before my knuckles ever made contact with the door of her condo. The last week, the pain, everything dissolved in the rush of our lips struggling to find each other's. The moment they met, rough against soft, determined and insistent, the dry, twisting ache in the center of my chest released.

I carried her inside, our mouths never parting, all the way to her bedroom. The fever dream that had been my drive from Princeton to Wilmington was swept away in my haste to remove shirts, shoes, jeans, bras, panties — all barriers to our bodies' union. We moved as if burning need would consume us both if we took longer than absolutely necessary.

My mouth searched for every part of her I could find, her hands and lips moving equally fast. Little noises came from both of us. We were a tangle of touching and stretching and reaching and doing our best to hold each other while fumbling onto the bed. Clothes off, condom on, and I pushed inside her, groaning in relief.

I couldn't decide if we were making love so much as fulfilling a basic need like eating or breathing. Having her again was like taking a cool drink of water after a hot day in the sun. We had to come together this way. I held her face, smoothing back her hair as I rocked into her body. Tears were in her eyes, but I kissed them away. Tears were in my eyes, but I closed them and kissed her more. All I knew was her. Her, me, passion, need, fulfillment, relief. It was amazing.

My hands moved from her face and hair to her breasts, which I pulled together to cover with my mouth, first one then the other as she sighed in response. My hands moved lower, cupping her ass, rocking her, as the tension between us grew tighter. Her hands caught my cheeks, lifting my hungry mouth to hers again. As soon as our lips met, she pushed my shoulder, and I rolled onto my back, her over me in a straddle, her hips rocking faster in her own rhythm.

She leaned forward, and I caught a taut nipple in my mouth again. She moaned, rocking her hips against me. Buried deep, I enjoyed the view of her slim torso, light blonde hair flicking around her shoulders. My fingers only lightly grazed her hips as she rode, coming faster until her body shook. Her moans turned to little cries and I thrust harder, allowing her inner squeezing to pull me with her.

Rolling her onto her back, I plunged hard and deep. Another satisfied sound, and my thrusting grew faster, stronger until I was coming, over and over, groaning against her beautiful neck, lost in the amazing sensation that was being buried inside the woman I loved, holding her in my arms.

Several hazy, glowing moments passed as we both recovered from our reunion. I rolled onto my back, but my arms wouldn't loosen their hold on her. I carried her with me, pulling her against my chest, her cheek pressed to my neck. Her arms were equally tight around me until at last our breath was calm, our hands were smoothing, caressing. I felt her lips touching my skin.

"Thank you for coming," she whispered.

"You always make me come." I couldn't resist.

She giggled and my arms tightened around her. "You know what I mean. That is not an easy drive."

"It's longer than I'd like, but I'm here now." I shrugged. I would've driven longer to be with her, to hold her this way.

My hands were on her back, and I couldn't stop massaging her skin, allowing her warmth and presence to ease every last bit of that wretched pain away. No more wondering what she was doing. No more wondering if she regretted saying goodbye as much as I regretted not stopping her. No more lying in bed at night hoping she was thinking of me, missing me as much as I missed her, hoping she hadn't gone back to him. One teary phone call removed all doubt.

She turned her face into my neck. "I can't believe I'm such a baby." Her voice was small, and I felt the tension rising in her body.

Rolling her onto her back again, I smoothed her hair off her cheeks and looked into her green eyes all stormy and troubled.

"What are you talking about?" I whispered, kissing her small nose, her chin.

Just like before, she touched my lips with her finger, and just like before, I kissed it. "I should've waited longer before I called you." Her slim brows pulled together, and she tried to turn away. But I wouldn't let her go. "It's only been a week. I didn't even attempt to get over you. All I could think about was holding you, touching you, you touching me. I caved after five days."

Suppressing a grin, I cupped her cheeks again and covered her mouth with mine. Her lips parted, and our tongues met. I felt her relaxing, and in that moment, the questions in my head were answered—and the answers satisfied me deeply. She was mine. No matter what came next. With a calm confidence, I knew I'd never let her go again.

My mouth moved to her cheek. "Nobody's getting over anybody here. So why torture us both?"

Her body shook with her small laugh. "Aren't you trained for torture?"

"Yes, but you're not."

She slid down and put her cheek against my chest again. "It's crazy trying to make this work," she sighed. "We barely know each other."

My fingers threaded into her silky hair. She was so beautiful in my arms. "I'd say we're off to a pretty good start. I'll take a chance if you will."

With her forehead rested on me, she sighed. "I still don't want a long distance relationship."

This time, nothing she said winded me like her words had in Scottsdale. Back then, I wasn't sure of anything. Now everything felt possible. I pushed against the mattress, sitting up and bringing her with me. Her green eyes glistened when they met mine, and I smiled.

"So we'll figure it out." I smoothed my thumbs over her cheeks. "We'll get through the weeks however we can, we'll be together on the weekends, and we'll figure out what the future's going to look like. This distance is not forever."

Her head dropped, but only for a moment. When she lifted it again, she moved forward, wrapping her arms around my neck. My hands spanned her waist before sliding up her body to cup her beautiful breasts. The scent of cactus flower surrounded me, and I lay her back, ready to catch up on all the days we'd missed.

"Now, that first time was amazing, but it went way too fast." I covered one tight nipple with my mouth and then the other as her little moans began, her fingers threaded in my hair.

"You think?" Her voice was breathless.

"Yes," I said against her body, traveling lower. I kissed her flat stomach, inhaling the warm perfume lingering on her skin. She whispered my name, and I gave her belly one more kiss before catching her thighs and spreading them open, sinking my tongue between her folds.

A low moan rose from her throat, shooting straight to my hardening cock. I pulled her closer to my mouth, tasting, sliding my fingers inside her, feeling her increasing wetness.

"Oh, Patrick," she gasped. Her back arched as her orgasm grew, as I sucked, pulled and licked her clit. I wasn't leaving that spot until she was screaming my name.

My tongue circled again and again, and her hips, her whole body, rotated with it. A few more pulls, and she was crying out, bucking against me. Pushing away, but pulling me closer, her fingers curling in my hair. My erection ached as I fumbled for my pants. I had to keep those damn condoms closer. Finding one, I ripped it open and managed to get it in place, sinking into her again while her muscles were still working.

She caught my cheeks, pulling my mouth to hers, finding my tongue as my dick plunged into her hot opening over and over. Her moans were muffled by our kisses. I broke away, groaning as I sank inside her. Instinct took over, and I went deeper, faster, as she held on, rocking her hips with mine.

Through the haze, I noticed her fingers on my ass, touching, exploring as her mouth burned a trail down my neck, her small tongue tasting before she bit my skin. The small pain registered directly to my cock, prompting more deep thrusts until I was gone, pounding her hard, flooding that condom. My whole body shook until finally I collapsed, spent, breathing hard against her hair, her fingers still moving on my ass.

Finally, I reached back and caught those wrists, holding both her wandering hands together over her head. The position pulled her breasts together in perky rounds beneath me, and I couldn't help it. I leaned down and caught one in my mouth, giving it a little suck, prompting a moan, before rising up to look at her again.

"What were you doing?"

"Mmm," she sighed, that little glint in her eye as she grinned up at me. "Playing with you."

"You bit me."

A tiny giggle slipped from her throat. "You came hard."

I kissed her for that. "You're amazing, and you're crazy in the sack, and I love it."

She laughed, that gorgeous sound I hadn't heard in a week, and lifted her lips to mine again. I released her hands, and she caught my neck, roughly claiming my mouth before breaking away. "Shall I tie you up again?"

My forehead dropped to her shoulder as I laughed. "How about we save that for a night when I'm not so tired." I might've resisted initially, but the memory of that blazing hot fuck was imprinted in my brain. We'd be going down that road again, I was sure of it.

She exhaled a contented sound, pushing me onto my back and resting her head on my shoulder. "I guess you're right. There's no point fighting this."

"That's my girl," my hand smoothed her back. "We'll be together as much as we can, and we'll work out the distance problem as soon as possible."

Exhaustion was creeping in, causing my eyes to grow heavy. Releasing a week of painful tension in bed with her after that long drive, all of it was hitting me hard, but I didn't want to be the dick who fell asleep the minute I got what I wanted.

"How was Back to School?" I said, suppressing a yawn.

Elaine turned, and I saw her covering an enormous yawn of her own. Of course, I laughed.

"Sorry!" she said, shaking her head. "It was fine, but damn, I'm exhausted."

Warmth flooded the place in my heart that for days had been a cold, dry ache. "Let's get some sleep then."

She curled around, pressing her back against my chest, and my arms went tight around her. After all we'd shared, it felt inevitable to have her this way. Her body drew me in until my heart beat with hers, and my soul felt threaded to her very breath. My lips pressed against her neck, then behind her ear. She was amazing.

"I'll tell you all about it tomorrow." Her voice was growing quieter, and I kissed the top of her shoulder, surrendering to sleep. I was back in heaven, and I wasn't leaving this place or my angel ever again.

## CHAPTER 14:
## THEN I MET YOU

The sound of plates clanging together woke me. I was alone in the bed, and it sounded like Elaine was rearranging the kitchen. A smile immediately curled my lips, and I hopped up, hitting the bathroom to lose the wood before stepping into my jeans and heading to where she was.

"What are you doing in here?" my brow creased as I took in the pots and pans scattered around my lady, who was dressed in a short white gown. It was lacy and showed off her body in the most incredible way. Morning wood returning.

She glanced up and her shoulders dropped. "I'm sorry," she said, stepping over a pot to kiss my cheek. "I didn't mean to wake you. I wanted to serve you breakfast in bed, but I can't find my damn omelet pan."

Catching her waist, I pulled her closer to me, kissing her temple, the side of her ear before whispering, "I'll take you out for breakfast."

Her body relaxed, and I felt her smile. "Have some coffee at least." She stepped around to pick up a glass pot sitting on the counter as I admired her body under that nearly sheer nightie.

"I'll just have some juice," I said, going to the fridge. "Got any?"

"Yeah, help yourself," she said, distracted as she put the pans back in the cabinet.

My phone buzzed from the center of the bar, and I realized I'd pretty much just walked out of the office yesterday afternoon. Derek probably thought something had happened. I grabbed the OJ and reached for a glass in the rack. Leaning against the sink, my phone buzzed again, and she glanced at it.

"You're getting a text," she said, lifting the small coffee pot and pouring the dark brown liquid in her mug.

"Is it Derek?" I took a long drink, not worried. "He probably thinks I had a family emergency or something the way I left yesterday."

Her brow creased, and she turned her head to read the face. "It's Kenny. He wants to know if Fatal Attraction got you." Her green eyes were hesitant as they rose to mine. "What's that about?"

Fuck. I did not want any of that coming into my space with Elaine. I put the glass down and stepped to the bar, picking up my phone and quickly texting back. *All good. Will catch up ASAP.*

"Sorry," I said, putting the phone back down and reaching for her. But I could tell she was still thinking about it. "It's stupid bullshit at work. I'm handling it."

"Fatal Attraction?" her brow arched. "Wasn't that about an office affair gone psycho?"

She had a right to be worried. I'd been a dick, and I was so lucky I'd met this amazing woman who saved me from myself.

"I called it that, but I was exaggerating. It was just this temp we had weeks ago. She's gone now."

"A temp?" Her expression caused the tension to burn in my stomach again. Elaine was so important to me. She was still standing in my arms, and I tightened my hold on her waist.

"I was an idiot," I said. "Then I met you."

I wasn't sure if she would even understand the enormous change those eight words conveyed, but I didn't know how else to put it. My phone buzzed again, and both our eyes went to it. Kenny.

*You were supposed to check in. Asshole.*

My lips tightened. I wasn't sure what to say, but everything changed when Elaine snorted a laugh. "You should at least tell him you're okay."

Relief washed over me, and I pulled her close, resting my forehead on hers. "I'd rather be okay with you," I said, kissing her lightly.

Her arms wrapped around my neck and she kissed me back. "Didn't you just promise to buy me breakfast?"

"I don't know if it was a promise. And this little dress you've got on is seriously pitching my tent."

She laughed and kissed me harder. Her response was not cooling my erection, but she let go, skipping back and going to her room. "Then I'd better change because I'm hungry."

Shaking my head, I picked up my phone and quickly typed back. *My bad. Sorry. Will explain soon.*

Returning the phone to the bar, I went to the bedroom. Elaine was already sliding faded jeans over her slim hips. Was it possible that everything this woman did turned me on?

"I need to stop at a drugstore," I said, picking up my shirt and buttoning it. "I didn't bring anything with me."

She turned, now wearing a long-sleeved navy tee with her jeans, and I watched as she shoved her feet into a pair of hot pink Chucks. "We'll take care of it. First, breakfast!"

I couldn't stop smiling as she caught my hand, pulling me to the door.

\* \* \*

The weekend was too short. Sitting at my desk in Princeton Monday morning, all I could do was gaze out the window, imagining myself in the car, flying to meet her again.

We'd spent the entire weekend either making love, chatting, eating, or sleeping. We'd told each other everything. I knew all about Brian The Idiot. The complete moron she'd dated five years who was so clueless he'd never proposed. Of course, I wasn't complaining. And I'd told her about Stacy.

Looking back on those relationships in view of what we shared, it was hard to believe they had ever seemed so important. What was more believable was how easily they ended. Nothing could last that didn't feel like this.

"I suppose it's chemistry?" Elaine's fingers had traced a delicate line along my cheek, down my jaw. I'd held her body tight under mine on the soft bed. It was my all-time favorite way to hold her.

Leaning down to kiss her chin, I answered. "Some people are just meant to be." I kissed her again, tasting her sweet mouth. "I've never felt this way about anyone in my life."

Her lips curled into a smile as she wrapped those lovely arms around my neck. "That's always nice to hear."

Kisses led to more lovemaking, and when it was time for me to go, it hurt like hell. But it wasn't devastating. The separation sucked, but everything was right now. I was back at work, smiling in anticipation of seeing her again, and I could actually concentrate on cracking the two cases in front of me while I passed the time.

Turning back to my computer, I began the process — scrolling through face after face, looking for Star's. I'd spend an hour on this, and if I didn't find her, I'd switch back to the phishing case for a while. Then I'd return to finding the needle in the haystack.

A cry from the kitchen broke my concentration. "Gross!" It was Nikki, and I was just about to tune her out when her words registered in my brain. "Who put plates and glasses in the dishwasher and didn't run it? This looks a month old!"

My brow creased. I didn't even know we had a dishwasher, and I was out of my chair in an instant. Derek wouldn't have done it — there was only one other possibility between Nikki leaving and coming back...

"Stop!" I shouted, freezing her hand just before it reached one of the glass tumblers I recognized from that Friday afternoon in my office.

Nikki stepped back, and I looked all around the kitchen for anything I could pick it out with. "Hurry up, it stinks!" She was holding her nose.

"Hang on." I dashed back down the hall to our supply closet. A neglected box of medical gloves was in the back corner, and I shoved my hand inside, pulling one out and snapping it on.

Back in the break room, I reached into the dishwasher, carefully lifting the glass that had remnants of beige lip gloss—and hopefully a decent fingerprint—lightly by the edge.

"Cross your fingers," I whispered, returning to my office.

Fingerprinting was as basic as addition in our line of work. I hoped to find something useable, and if I did, I hoped it led to answers. I took out the small kit I hadn't touched in years and dipped the soft brush in the feathery, black powder. It was a pretty old-school technique, and not something I did very often. Dusting all around the edge, several smears readily appeared, but nothing distinct. I kept coating, but still nothing showed up. My chest sank. I was on the verge of quitting, when I took one more pass under the lip gloss smudge. Jackpot. A thumbprint stood out, and I almost shouted. Then I remembered Derek didn't know I was working on this case, so I stood and crossed my office, shutting the door.

A clear piece of tape over the print, and in moments, I was attaching it to a blank sheet of printer paper. There it was, clear as day. Turning back to my computer, I took the sheet and fed it into our scanner. Once I had the image, all I had to do was submit it to Fieldprint and wait. I'd have the location of Star Brandon in hours. Less time if I was lucky. My chest tightened in anticipation. I couldn't wait to get to the bottom of this.

## Chapter 15:
## One to Keep

Star Brandon was not a real name.

No surprises there, even Nikki called that one, but what did surprise me was the only record anybody had of her was as Toni Durango of Raleigh, North Carolina. I shook my head at the additional, obviously fake name, and wondered if the work address, The Skinniflute bar, was equally false.

It was clearly her photo, beside a two-year old arrest record for indecent exposure. Seemed Ms. Durango thought a thong bikini would be acceptable in Myrtle Beach, but the conservative residents thought otherwise. The charges had eventually been dropped, but it gave me a place to start. If that turned up nothing, Tom Brandon was my next search. He'd given her his name and called her, perhaps he was her boss.

My mind scrolled through the possibilities, the most pleasant of which was that I'd have an excuse to be in

Elaine's home state again. I heard Derek's voice—he said my name loudly, but then it tapered off. Fine with me, I wanted to read every word of the Star/Toni report and note any clues it might give me to her current whereabouts.

The noises out in the hallway grew louder. I glanced at my closed door. A female voice was speaking rapidly, but I didn't recognize it. It wasn't Nikki. Star/Toni's information was still up on my screen, as I slowly stood, finishing the page.

The voice tapered off as I opened my door. That's when it sounded vaguely familiar. I was out in the hallway just in time to see the front glass doors closing and Derek standing at the entrance to his office looking shell-shocked. He quickly went after whoever that was, but when he went out, the foyer was empty. I followed him.

"Are you okay?" He didn't even look at me. Without a word, he turned and went back into his office. "Derek. What happened?" My concern was growing by the second.

He walked straight to the windows and looked down, turning his head as if he were trying to see something. I looked down, too, but all I saw was the empty courtyard below. For several minutes he simply stood watching, not speaking. My brow creased as I studied his face—lined, dark brow furrowed, blue eyes full of pain.

"What happened?" I repeated.

Nikki stepped into the room and quickly crossed to him, touching his arm. Her voice was quiet, gentle. "Was that her?" she asked.

My mind flew through everything that just happened—everything I wasn't paying attention to.

Derek had said my name then his voice cut off. Several minutes passed, and I heard that female voice... I noticed Derek's jaw clench, and he turned back to the desk, quickly sitting behind it. I looked at Nikki, but she shook her head.

"What *her* do you mean?" I asked.

"Melissa was just here." My partner's dead tone immediately caused me to sit.

"Melissa?" I repeated. "But... why?" Clearly it hadn't gone well.

Elbows bent, Derek put his face in his hands, his fingers pushing back the dark hair. For several seconds he stayed that way, and I sat watching him, waiting. My eyes scanned his desk. A small pouch lay on top of some papers, otherwise, nothing unusual was in front of him.

Nikki's voice was hesitant. "Is there anything I can do?" She carefully reached out and put her hand on his arm.

Dropping his hands, Derek cleared his throat, turned to his computer, and started typing. I watched in silence as he pulled up the state government site for Maryland and started scrolling.

"Want to tell me what happened?" I tried again.

I knew his longing for Melissa was as powerful as mine had been for Elaine. Now that I'd had my need met, I felt better about offering to help. I wasn't walking around like a hollowed-out shell of a person anymore.

The telephone out front beeped and Nikki left the room. Her voice in the reception area echoed back to us, and Derek slowly turned to face me.

"He beat her." His voice was quiet.

"What?" I slid forward in the chair, anger rising in my stomach. "Melissa? Who beat her?"

I didn't know her very well, but I knew her well

enough. I knew Derek loved her, and I knew she was Elaine's best friend. If someone had hurt her, I'd gladly help Derek kick the shit out of him and put him away — in whatever order they preferred. But I was confused. Derek didn't seem ready to act.

"Her husband." Still quiet, his voice now sounded broken. "I didn't know. I didn't even check."

A flash like white light hit my face. "Melissa's married? But I thought you two were—"

"I knew her husband from Princeton. He hired me to follow her to Scottsdale. To see if she was having an affair. I told him she wasn't."

This revelation had me slowly sliding back in my chair again. I watched Derek as he spoke. He'd never struck me as the homewrecker type, and I knew how he felt about sleeping with clients. Now he was telling me this potentially explosive story of how he'd broken all his rules.

"Did he beat her when he found out?" I asked, unsure how to proceed. Cheating or not, abuse was still unacceptable to me.

"No," he said. "It was before. Apparently a while back. It's why she was leaving him. She'd filed for divorce before she went to the desert. He lied to me."

I was sure the confusion was clear on my face. I didn't know anything about the case that had taken him to Arizona, and now I was learning he'd been hired by Melissa's almost-ex-husband to investigate her, and he'd ended up falling in love with her.

"Is this why you blamed me?" I asked, remembering his demeanor at the bar, his incomplete story.

Weary blue eyes lifted to mine, and I decided to drop all comparisons to my screw up or how this pretty much got me off the hook.

"Explain this abuse part," I said. "What was that about?"

He picked up the small pouch on his desk and opened it, lifting out a gold chain with a small floating heart on it. "She thinks I knew. She thinks I helped him knowing what he'd done to her." His fist closed around the delicate piece of jewelry, and he lifted it to his lined brow. "I've got to fix this."

Derek stood quickly, heading down the hall to an older storage closet that contained several filing cabinets. In a few moments he was back carrying a file. I sat watching.

"What are you doing?" I asked.

"She said he hired prostitutes." He seemed recharged. "Abusers usually have a pattern. I need to find another woman he hurt."

"This guy sounds like a real winner." I couldn't keep the sarcasm out of my voice. "You didn't know about any of this?"

He shook his head, quietly scanning the pages. The folder had the name *Reynolds* on it, and I remembered it was the name Melissa had said at dinner that night. Her former marketing client. Derek stood and snatched his suit coat off the back of his chair along with his keys and phone.

"I might be out of the office a few days," he said, going to the door. "Nikki, forward my calls and emails."

He pushed out the glass doors, and the office was suddenly quiet. Staring after him, I processed all he'd said. It was an awful story. It was what had taken him to the desert. Melissa and Elaine were out there together on a spa vacation—a mental health break, Elaine had said.

If Melissa thought Derek was lying to her, had she told Elaine what happened? I was on my feet and headed to my office in an instant. Shutting my door, I grabbed my phone and touched her number. Elaine had to know I didn't know shit about any of this.

\* \* \*

Nine hours later, Elaine's body was back beneath mine, my arms tight around her waist, and I was breathing an enormous, internal sigh of relief. Moments before she'd been crying out in ecstasy, but before all of that, she'd been about to hit me and throw me out of her condo.

Again, an enormous, internal sigh of relief.

After Derek had left to do God knows what about his situation with Melissa, I'd tried calling Elaine. When my third call went to voicemail, I knew something was wrong. Scooping up my things, I went straight to my car headed for Wilmington. Nikki followed me into the hall complaining about Alexander and Knight both disappearing at once, but I wasn't listening. Whatever my senior partner had done, I'd be damned if he cost me the woman I loved. I drove all eight hours thinking of what I might say, which wasn't going to be much, considering I'd just found out about the whole thing.

Apparently, Elaine had been in the car while Melissa had been in our offices. She was just getting home after dropping her friend off at her new place when I met her.

"I'm not ready to see you now, Patrick," she said, attempting to push me out of the house.

I caught her hands, not letting her go. "You can't shut me out. I didn't know anything about what Derek was doing."

She was still trying to push me out, but the more she pushed, the more I held on until she finally stopped struggling. Still, her green eyes flashed with anger.

"He only told me it was complicated," I said. "Then when we got back, all I could think about was you. I didn't pay any attention to his cases."

"You're trying to tell me you two are in the same office and you never discuss your work?"

"Baby, I promise…" I reached for her waist, but she blocked my hands.

"Don't *baby* me. I want the truth, Patrick Knight. Melissa's been through hell, and I won't waste time on players who have no respect for women."

"I respect you." My fingers threaded with hers, and I pulled her to me. "And I believe you. I'm sorry about what happened with Melissa. Fuck, I want to kill that guy." My voice grew softer. "Please believe me when I promise you, I didn't know about any of it until today. Derek was seriously playing it all close to the vest. Probably to protect her."

Her lips were still a tight line, but she was in my arms now. My muscles were starting to unclench, and when she lowered her head to my chest, they completely relaxed. I kissed her head and she turned her cheek to the side, pressing it against my heart.

"She's so hurt," Elaine said, her voice cracking. "I've never seen her so devastated. Even after it happened. I know she's still in love with him."

My hands rubbed her slim back. "Her husband?"

"No." She shook her head. "Derek. Melissa loves Derek. She barely spoke the whole drive home, and I think she was just holding on until she could be alone and fall apart."

"We'll check on her," I said, moving my hands down to her waist. She was wearing a black skirt, and a sleeveless black top that was slightly cropped, exposing a half inch of her lined torso. She was so beautiful. "Let's make up first."

"I'm not sure if I'm ready." She stepped back, but I caught her hand, bringing her back to me.

"Look," I said, catching her chin and raising her eyes to mine. "I love you, and I'll do whatever I can to help Derek bring that guy down. He's already started working on it, building a case."

Her expression changed as I spoke, and the look in her eyes—happiness combined with wonder—melted me.

"What did you just say?" she asked, eyes shining.

I tried to remember. I replayed my words in my head until I realized it. *Shit*. My jaw clenched, but I didn't answer. I hadn't meant to say that out loud yet.

"Patrick?" her voice was soft, almost a whisper and this time she caught my chin with her slim hand, forcing my eyes to meet hers.

"I called you baby," I said, a grin touching my lips. "I know you love that."

"That wasn't all you said." Her voice was lower and she rose on her toes, putting her face closer to mine. Her arms wrapped around my neck and we were a breath apart, noses almost touching. The scent of her delicate perfume surrounded me, and her lips parted. I barely moved, covering them with mine, mouths opening, tongues curling together.

In a flash she was off her feet and in my arms. I carried her back to the bedroom, and we were on the bed, her hands working at my belt, my hand fishing in my pocket for protection. Soon enough I was rocking into her, her legs wrapped around my waist, any disagreement between us forgotten.

162

Which brought us back to the lovely moment of her body under mine. We were still partially dressed, but I'd managed to get her out of that black top and bra. Her skirt was another matter, bunched around her waist. My shirt was still on my shoulders, but it was open, allowing her breasts to be flush with my skin. I kissed her temple, her eyebrow, her nose.

"What was it you said before?" Her eyes sparkled as she repeated the question from earlier.

I couldn't help but smile. "I don't know what you mean."

"I think you do."

With a deep breath, I gave in and said it.

"I love you, Elaine Merritt. I love your eyes and your laugh and the way your lips feel against mine." It was all coming out now in a rush, and I wasn't stopping it. "I love how smart you are and how much you care about your students. I love that you'll protect your friends. I love your independence…"

Her chin lifted with her laugh, and she pulled her body closer to mine. "I'm not so independent," she said, kissing my jaw. "I couldn't go a whole week without you."

"I'm so glad you couldn't," I said, pressing my lips to hers again briefly. "I love making love to you. I just… I love you."

It was the first time I'd said it to any woman not related to me since Stacy, but it was so right. It was so much more than that near-mistake, that injury that had left me going down a self-destructive path. That had led me here.

My heart was something I'd gladly give her. I'd given it to her already, she just didn't know. I was afraid it was too soon, yet everything leading us to this point solidified my decision.

For a moment, she only looked at me, that beautiful smile on her face. Then she pulled her body up, placing her mouth close to my ear. "I love you, Patrick Knight." Her soft lips touched my skin. "I love you so much."

My eyes closed as my arms tightened around her. Whatever happened between us, in that moment, I knew the truth. She was my heart and my soul. She was the one I'd never get over. She was the one I would always keep.

## CHAPTER 16:
### FUCKED-UP LOGIC

Raleigh was not on the way to Wilmington, but as soon as I finished my business there, all I could think about was spending the night in Elaine's arms. She didn't know about this trip—nobody did. I was making the drive south to wrap up an unpleasant chapter in my life she didn't need to worry about. It was the last possible obstacle to our happy future.

The "Skinny" biker bar was about what I expected—a low dive with the standard dark-wood exterior. It was happy hour, and several hogs were lined up out front. I parked the Charger around the corner and walked to the entrance. My blazer was in the backseat, so all I had on were jeans and a short-sleeve black tee. For once, I wished my hair was darker. If I'd cut it shorter, it would be more brown, but Elaine liked it shaggy.

We were close enough to summer that the natural highlights still had me looking like the surfer walking into the biker bar. It was a stupid cliché, but I should be okay. Derek and I were still working out pretty regularly, and the ink on my arms was exposed. Along with the deeper cut-lines. I might look young, but I could kick ass if I had to. And anyway, trouble wasn't what I wanted. I was after information.

Inside the place was dim-lit with neon signs scattered around the walls. A few big guys sat at the dark-wood bar that had metal plates lining the front. They all wore standard denim and leather biker outfits, and in addition to their long hair, they had bandannas around their heads. All of them had full beards, and none of them paid any attention to me.

A game was on the small television hanging in the corner, holding their gaze. At the pool table in the back, a few younger guys were cuing up. I took a seat at the wooden booth across from the jukebox, which was silent. I'd give it a few drinks before trying to mingle.

It only took a minute before a stacked waitress wearing frayed denim shorts and a white tank top came to my table. Her dark hair was tied in a ponytail with a red bandanna, and she wore too much black eye makeup around her brown eyes.

"What can I get you?" she asked, allowing her gaze to travel over my body. Her confident assessment of my physique gave me an idea.

"Vodka. Up," I said, sitting back and flipping out a twenty. "And some info."

Her eyebrow arched, and she picked up the bill. "I'll bring your change for the drink. Tell me what you want to know, and I'll tell you the price."

Turning on her heel, she walked lazily back to the bar. A small round tray was perched on her hand, and her ass wasn't too bad, swaying as she moved. I figured she got all the action she wanted at this place.

Three minutes, and she returned with my drink. "My break's in a half-hour. We can talk then."

"What's your name?" I took the drink and my change, leaving a few singles behind for her.

"Lylah," she said, cocking her hip to the side. Only thing this girl was missing was the gum.

"Thanks, Lylah," I said, taking a sip. "I look forward to it."

The bar continued to fill as the minutes passed. A few guys smoked, reviving the stale scent already in the place, and the pool area was now full. Some played, most watched, all had longnecks. A guy fed the jukebox, and classic rock joined the noise. It wouldn't be too long before I got the full Skinniflute experience.

Lylah showed up at what must've been a half hour later and slid into the booth across from me. "Where you from?" she asked, tapping a cigarette out of a box, which she then tilted in my direction.

I held up a hand. "No thanks. Princeton."

She shrugged and lit it, leaning back against the booth as she took a long drag. "So what's a pretty college boy like you doing in this dump?"

I'd let her think what she wanted about my occupation. "How long have you worked here?"

"About a year." She blew a long exhale of blue smoke as she said it. "Moved up from the coast when I was eighteen."

My insides tightened at that revelation. Could it be this easy? "Which one?"

She blinked, but answered. "Charleston."

Yeah, it was too much to hope she might've said Myrtle Beach.

I picked up my vodka and took another sip, thinking.

"Is that all you wanted to know?" she frowned. "That info can be on the house."

"I'm just looking for someone, but I don't know if you can help me."

She took another long drag. "Your wife?"

I smiled and shook my head. "No."

"Yeah, you're too young and shiny to be married."

Little did she know I almost was. "Ever heard of someone named Durango?"

"Oh, sure." She said it so casually, my stomach clenched. "Toni came back a month ago. Got sick of following Ron around."

She exhaled another long puff as my brow creased. I knew a Ron, but if it was the same guy, I was still stumped. I'd never done anything to him.

"Well, my break's over," she said, scooting out of the booth. "If you're not a cop, I won't charge you for the intel."

"I'm not a cop," I said, my hand resting on the short glass, which was now empty.

"Want me to freshen that?"

I glanced up at her then. "Sure. Thanks."

She took the tumbler and headed back to the bar in the center of the place. The crowd seemed as big as it was going to get on this Thursday night, and Lylah returned much quicker this time with my refill.

"I'm almost done for tonight, but I've got some good news for you." She leaned forward as she set the glass on the table.

"Yeah?" I only glanced briefly at the cleavage shot she was giving me. I'd be with Elaine tomorrow.

"Toni's on the schedule for tonight. She'll be in at nine."

Adrenaline kicked in. The Budweiser clock hanging on the wall behind her said eight-fifteen. "Thanks," I said, putting an extra twenty on her tray. "Keep it."

Her eyebrow went up and she smiled. White teeth behind red lips. "Thanks...?"

She waited, and I thought about my answer. If she told Toni I was here, that might not help me.

"Brian," I said, giving her a wink. Elaine's ex was the first name that popped into my head.

"Thanks, Brian. I'll tell her you're looking for her."

I nodded, opting not to do anything suspicious like tell her not to say anything. There was no reason to think a Brian looking for Toni would make her run.

* * *

Half-way through nursing my second vodka, I saw a new waitress enter behind the bar. I couldn't see her face, but her hair was long and now dark brown, similar to Lylah's, only this one wore hers in a side ponytail. She had on silver hotpants with silver heels, and I recognized both the shoes and that ass. Anger tightened in my stomach at the memory, but I kept my cool. She'd done a job, and I needed to know why and for whom. If it was Ron, I hoped she'd at least point me to him.

I waited, watching as she tied on a little black pocketed apron and picked up a small round tray. I didn't see Lylah, and figured Toni had no idea I was here—or Brian was here—looking for her. She stopped and talked to the big guys still sitting at the bar. They'd been here longer than me and seemed to be regulars from the way they laughed and joked. Her hair was different, but I also knew that smile. She still wore beige glossy lipgloss, and her bangs hung in her black-lined brown eyes. It was all too familiar.

After another five minutes, she said something to the men at the bar and turned to make a pass through the room. She started at the pool area, gave the guys there a brief wave before turning around and facing me. Our eyes met and she froze on the spot.

Hers widened and then quickly narrowed, and she slowly walked to where I sat. The fact that she wasn't even afraid to approach me after what happened spoke volumes about who I was dealing with. This female was a pro. She stopped at the wooden booth right in front of me and put a hand on her hip.

"What do you want, Mr. Knight?" Her voice was that same low purr I remembered.

"Have a seat?" I said, motioning to the empty spot across from me. A glance flickered to it, and she stowed the tray on the top of the booth, sliding across the glossy wooden bench.

For a moment, I only looked at her. She obviously dabbled in the business, and I must've been one fucked up shithead not to see it. Vodka would do that to a person. My eyes went to the half-full glass in front of me.

"I'd offer to buy you a drink, but I guess you're on the clock." I couldn't resist being familiar. She'd had my dick in her mouth after all.

Her lips curled slightly. "You went through a lot of trouble to find me. Is this your way of saying you want more?"

"No." I tilted the glass, deciding just to say it. "Who hired you and why."

She leaned back, studying me. "What makes you think I'd just tell you something like that?"

"I want to know who's messing with me."

"Go through your list." She gave the room a quick, visual sweep. The patrons all seemed fine for now. "Haven't you made any enemies?"

"Trust me, I've got assholes out there who'd like to get back at me, but sending you around is something special."

She smiled, fixing those dark eyes on me again. "I'll take that as a compliment."

"Take it however you want it. You did your job. I want to know who sent you."

"I've got to get back to work." She stood, but I stood with her, catching her forearm and not letting her leave.

"What do you want for it?" I said quietly.

She leaned closer, glancing down at my mouth. "You're pretty special yourself." She used the seductive voice that now turned my stomach. "I'm off at two—"

"Not interested." I released her arm. "What's up with you and Ron?"

Her eyes flashed then, and she stepped back. "Who told you about me and him?"

"Looks like you just did."

Her hand lifted, but I caught it. "I wouldn't start slapping now. Did Ron hire you?"

"No." She jerked away from my grip. "His sister. She paid me five hundred dollars to teach you a lesson."

My head spun at that response. "Stacy hired you?"

I momentarily lost focus as one question consumed my thoughts: Why would my ex-fiancé use her low-life younger brother to hire a call girl to seduce me? Half a grand to teach me a lesson? It didn't make any sense.

At the same time, it had to be true. How else would Toni connect me to Ron's sister?

"I never work for so cheap," Toni continued, "but they said I could do as much or as little as I wanted."

My eyes snapped to hers. "Which did I get?"

"Oh, you're sweet." Her brow arched. "You got the works."

"And the crazybitch act?"

She exhaled deeply, twisting her lips into a frown. "Ron thought it'd be funny to scare you a little. Said you'd really hurt his sister. That wasn't my idea."

"So I got a bonus lesson."

"I'm sorry—"

"Save it." I wasn't hearing any more of her shit. "What was the original lesson?"

"You'll have to ask Ron. I only did what they told me to do." She paused, watching my face. "He's here in Raleigh if you want to see him."

My attention returned to her, and her expression had changed. The faintest hint of compassion softened her tough-girl demeanor.

"You look pretty shook up," she said, but I didn't care. I was confused and pissed as I watched her pull a thick order pad from one of her pockets and scribble out an address. She ripped off the top sheet and handed it to me. "Ron's a dickwad. I don't care if you tell him I sent you."

I folded the paper and stuffed it in my back pocket. "Thanks," I said, dropping cash on the table and heading for the exit. She said something more, but I wasn't listening. My brain was too distracted by this unexpected turn of events, and I was ready for her to be a thing of the past. I was ready for all of this to be explained and then gone. A freakin bizarre-assed blip on my radar screen.

* * *

I'd met Stacy's brother Ron once on a dinner date in Chicago. He was high the entire time, and Stacy was worried I'd do something. But I didn't have any intention of busting one of my fiancée's close family members. Looking back, it all seemed so stupid.

The cinder-block shack Toni sent me to off Highway 1 was painted light blue and reminded me of something you might see abandoned near the beach. The yard was nothing but weeds and scrub, and sheets hung over the small windows. I parked the Charger in the driveway next to a beat-up Cobra and walked around to the side entrance facing the street. Cars shot by, and the door looked like I could kick it in without much effort. I was about ready to kick something in. Instead I banged and waited.

Several minutes passed, but I still waited. If Ron was anything like I remembered, it was no telling what was happening behind this closed door. Finally, I beat on it again, this time harder, and sounds came from inside. Two seconds and the door jerked open in a crack. My hand shot out and pushed it all the way open hard.

"What the fuck?" Ron stumbled back squinting. He wore jeans that barely stayed on his hips and a dirty white tee. I stepped into the dim room that reeked of cigarettes, pot, and burritos. "What the hell, man?" he continued.

I didn't have time for his shit. I was ready to get this over with and be with Elaine. Lose this bad memory in her soft skin and sweet perfume.

"Do you remember me?" I demanded.

It was possible he didn't because for one, he was out of his mind when we met, and for two, I was slightly

173

bigger now thanks to Derek's "kill the pain" weight-lifting regimen.

Without a word, Ron jerked around, trying to make a break for the back exit, but I caught him easily in one lunge.

"I can get your money by tomorrow," he whined. "Just give me twelve hours."

I had him by the neck, so I gave him a good shake. I wanted to punch him in the face, but I wanted him to talk first.

"Idiot," I growled. "You don't owe me money. I'm Patrick Knight. Stacy's ex."

His dirty hand passed over his lined face, and then he threw an elbow at me, twisting as he tried to escape my grip.

"Let me go, motherfucker," he yelled, no longer the sniveling idiot he was half a second ago.

I held on and shook him harder. "Why did Stacy send Toni Durango to me?" He flailed again, and it was all I could do to keep from kicking his sorry ass. "Stop struggling and tell me."

He tried one more time, and my grip tightened on his neck. Whining, he dropped to his knees. "You're hurting me, man."

"What was the lesson?"

"Stacy said you didn't give her a chance." He was spilling his guts fast. "She said she wanted a hot chick to teach you a lesson. That's all I know."

I let him go with a shove. "That doesn't make any fucking sense!" I yelled. Ron lay on the floor now, and my leg was itching to kick him. But I held back. "A lesson for what? She cheated on me."

He crawled over to the couch and pulled himself into a sitting position. Then he reached for a soft pack of cigarettes and pulled one out. I watched as he lit up, inhaling deeply and then blowing out a long stream of smoke.

"That's just it," he said. "She wants to get you back."

Rubbing my eyes, I turned to the door. "For what?"

"No, man, she *wants* you back. She wants you to be together again."

Not so long ago, those words would've affected me. Even after Kenny, and our supposed "rebound sex," I would've cared that Stacy wanted me back. Now everything was different.

"That logic is about as fucked up as you are," I said, pulling the cheap door open and inhaling the fresher outside air.

"You should call her," Ron yelled after me, but I slammed that door shut.

It was late, and I wanted nothing more than to drive to Wilmington and spend the night holding Elaine in my arms. But I was mad, and I smelled like old cigarettes. And I had to get to the bottom of this bullshit first. So instead of going back to heaven, I drove to the nearest Hyatt and got a room.

## CHAPTER 17:
### CHANGING EVERYTHING

Stacy's voice sounded the same as it always had — light and breezy, like a Saturday afternoon by the lake. I could still remember how that sound used to make me feel back when I thought she was worth having. I lay on the king-sized bed staring at the ceiling as I listened. It was ten o'clock, and I had the room until noon. I wanted to finish this now, shower, and then get on the road to Wilmington. It was only a two-hour drive to Elaine, and she'd be almost finished with her teaching day when I got there.

"I've thought about you a lot," Stacy said, but her disembodied voice on the line wasn't enough for me.

The entire Star episode and fallout, that it happened at my office, that she orchestrated the entire thing was too sharp in my memory. For a half-second, I wished I was back in Chicago having this conversation.

"Hang on," I said, sitting up. "I'm calling you back on video."

I ended the call and pulled out my tablet. I wanted to see her face when I heard her answer. Seconds later she appeared on the screen. Her blonde hair still ended at the tops of her shoulders in a little flip, and today she wore a pink sweater. Her brown eyes were open and hopeful, and I thought of how she'd looked the first time I saw her almost three years ago at the University of Chicago. I was fresh out of the military, starting a new chapter in my life, and she'd seemed perfect, a shiny premed student. I'd asked her out, and we'd spent two sweet years together, leading up to my proposal. Turns out sweet wasn't enough for her. Now I knew it wasn't enough for me, either.

"You look great," she said in that voice. "So beachy and fit."

"Thanks," I said. "You look... the same."

A little smile lifted the corner of her mouth. "What's on your mind?"

I was not smiling. "I talked to Ron last night. He said you wanted to get back together."

That made her brow crease. "You talked to Ron?" Her voice was not so Saturday at the lake now. "How is he?"

"He's the same loser he ever was, but I wanted to know if what he said was true."

Her forehead relaxed, and she gave me that smile again. "Well, I did tell him I've been thinking about you and us... How would you feel about that?"

"I might've felt something not so long ago," I said. "Now I just want to know what the lesson was."

"Lesson?" She blinked quickly. "What do you mean?"

"You'll have to tell me. Ron and Toni only know you were trying to teach me a lesson, but I guess I need to be in the slow class. I don't get it."

"This is all too cryptic for me." She fake-laughed. "I don't know what you're talking about."

"About three weeks ago, a foxy blonde call girl gave me the works. Then she tried to make me think she was married and psycho. She tried to rattle me." I said. "All of it was courtesy you."

"Did Ron tell you that?"

"Yes, and I believe him."

She shook her head. "Well, I don't know why. I have no idea what he's talking about. He probably wants drug money."

"Toni corroborated it, and she has no reason to know about our history."

"She's probably one of Ron's whores. They'll do anything he says." She sat back and looked away.

Irritation was stirring low in my gut, and my chest was growing tight with anger. I was sick of this.

"I would've agreed with you, but I saw them separately. Toni isn't doing your brother any favors. So cut the crap and tell me what message you're trying to send."

Her head snapped to the screen, and though we were miles apart, it felt like we were in the same room at that moment. "You said I wasn't worth the time of day." She dared to sound injured. "You called me a whore."

My jaw clenched, but I let her finish. I remembered how hurt and angry I'd been when I said those words.

"Now you know what it's like to be tempted. It's not so easy to say no when someone's coming on strong. When you're weak and not expecting it."

She seemed to be done, but I waited a few moments longer to be sure. When she still didn't speak, I nodded.

"So that's why you think what you did to me is okay?" I said, completely calm.

Her eyes blinked down to her lap. "I didn't say it was okay. I only said you should understand now."

I pressed my lips together as if that required any thought. "I understand that we were engaged when you cheated on me. I understand that I trusted you when you started screwing 24B. I also understand that when Toni appeared in my office, I was single and broken and still trying to recover from your lies."

She blinked up at those words. "But you don't have to recover!"

"You're damn right I don't. I have to thank you."

"Thank me?" The glimmer of hope on her face might've made this moment sweet if I still needed revenge. Somehow, I didn't anymore. Somehow, what she'd done didn't matter to me now. The fist in my chest had released, and I just wanted to say these last words and be done with her. For good.

"Thank you for removing any last feelings I might've had for you." Pausing a moment to check, I nodded as I recognized my insides were completely still. "You've shown me how I've changed. I am finally able to say I don't give a shit what you do. You're completely out of my system."

"But—"

"Have a nice life, Stacy." I reached forward and tapped the screen, ending the call. Then I stood, feeling whole again. Any unfinished business was completely wrapped up. If it were a real thing, I'd put a bow around it and drop it in the trash can.

Instead, I walked to the bathroom and started the shower. I was ready to scrub this trip from my body and wash it down the drain. Then I'd spend the weekend with the woman I did care about. The woman I loved.

\* \* \*

Holding Elaine in my arms made me feel like a lifetime had passed between what happened in Raleigh and now.

I'd arrived at her small, private school in time to see her in action before the day ended. Her principal had let me check in and go to her class, but Elaine didn't know I was there.

I stood outside the door, watching through the small window as she taught her class of sixth graders about literature and vocabulary and fantasy and romance. I couldn't help but smile as I watched her slowly go from desk to desk. She was so thoughtful working with them. Holding her long, blonde hair back, she leaned beside a boy's desk and pointed to a passage in the book. She said something to him then waited, her pretty brow lined, a concerned expression in her eyes, until he responded.

Whatever he said, her entire face beamed with pride and she nodded. I couldn't see the kid from where I stood, but I knew if that had been me at eleven, and I'd just made my hot teacher that proud, I would've been over the moon for the rest of the day. I couldn't help but grin.

Just as the bell rang, her eyes rose and met mine through the glass, and a different smile crossed her face. My stomach tightened in response, and I had to remind myself we were at school. I wanted to go through that door, pull her to me, and cover that pretty mouth with mine. Instead, I waited at the door, and once the kids were gone, she lunged forward, throwing her arms around my neck.

"What are you doing here?" she cried. "I thought I wasn't seeing you this weekend!"

I leaned down and kissed her softly. "I had some business to take care of in Raleigh, so I figured I'd stop by on my way back to Princeton."

Her sweet laugh filled the now-empty classroom. "This isn't on the way back."

My lips followed the line of her jaw to the side of her face, brushing her ear. "You think I'd be that close and not come to you?"

She shivered and turned her head to meet my mouth. Our tongues curled together, and I couldn't help the physical response her kiss evoked. She giggled, pressing her nose to my cheek. "We'd better head to my place before we get detention."

"Indecent exposure?" I said against her skin. For a moment, I pictured lifting her onto her desk, sliding her red skirt up and taking care of business.

"At the very least," she said, stepping away and picking up a case.

I waited as she slid three stacks of papers into it, followed by a computer tablet and a few books. She pushed a lock of light blonde hair behind her ear as she studied her phone.

"Something wrong?" I said, watching her progress.

"Melissa said she couldn't make the meeting at school today."

"Oh," I looked down with a sheepish grin. "That could be my fault. I bumped into her in the parking lot."

She blinked up to me. "What happened?"

I shrugged, catching her waist and pulling her to me again. Her hands went to my shoulders. "I might've suggested she consider giving Derek another chance." Elaine's eyes closed and she shook her head slowly.

"I know," I continued before she could speak. "But he still loves her. And I hate seeing the big guy hurting like that."

With a sigh, she rose up to kiss my cheek then stepped back to pull her case onto her shoulder. "I've tried telling her the same thing, but she'll have to come around on her own. She won't change just because we tell her to."

I nodded, following her out. "She's tough," I said. "Derek's met his match in the stubborn department."

She waved goodbye to a staff member and her principal made a joke about me remembering to call her as we went through the door.

"Were you flirting with Ms. Alvarez?" Elaine's eyes narrowed when we reached the car.

I leaned in for another quick kiss. "Only because I wasn't sure if she'd let me back to see you."

"I can't let you out of my sight."

"Yes, you can."

Now we were in her bed, bodies entwined, relaxed from an intense round of catch-up sex that had started on the kitchen counter and ended in the bedroom. I couldn't help but smile as I took in her flushed cheeks, her sparkling green eyes, shiny blonde hair spilling over the pillow beside me. I still couldn't believe this amazing creature came out of nowhere to be so right for me. How she'd barged into my life, snatched my heart, and changed everything.

"What are you thinking?" Her voice was soft as she leaned up to kiss my lips.

"How much I love you," I said, kissing her back.

She smiled and breathed a little laugh. "You are very charming, Mr. Knight."

"You are very sexy, Ms. Merritt." I leaned down to kiss her neck and noticed her breasts needed attention. Naturally, I slid down to kiss them as well.

"Mmm…" Her fingers slid through the sides of my hair, and I turned my face to rest my cheek against her heart, listening to it beating in her chest. Different, better, real.

* * *

Our weekends felt shorter every time we were together. On Sunday after breakfast, we went down to the shore before I had to leave again, and I could tell by her quiet mood, the distance was on her mind.

"What are you thinking?" I said, stopping our walk and pulling her into my arms.

She didn't answer at first. She placed her chin on my shoulder and looked out at the waves, the soft breeze blowing her hair back. I kissed her temple and whispered in her ear, "Tell me."

She met my gaze. "I was actually thinking about the school and my job."

"You're so good at it. I was very impressed."

A little smile crossed her lips. "I do love it, but I'm so distracted this year."

"Why?"

"My thoughts just go to the most unexpected places." My arms were still tight around her, and she shook her head, looking down. "There's a little boy, Cooper, in my class, and he has this light brown hair and hazel eyes. He's so cute, and every time I look at him, I catch myself thinking of you."

I kissed her cheek. "You want to play sexy teacher?"

"Not like that," she laughed a little, but her voice was thoughtful. "I think about how he could be yours."

I smiled and kissed her forehead. "I'm pretty sure I don't have any children."

"But you will."

"Wait..." The realization of what she was saying hit me then. "You're thinking about my children?"

Her cheeks turned the softest shade of pink. "I don't know," she said. "Cooper just made me think about it."

"When I get back I'm going to talk to Derek about relocating to Wilmington." The idea had been in my head, but I wasn't ready to say the words until now. "I'll get my own place, of course."

"What?" Her brow was lined, but her eyes were shining. "You'd do that?"

"Yes." Nothing had ever felt more certain in my life. "I like the coast, I can telecommute easily —"

A smile curled the side of her mouth. "You like the coast? That's your reason?"

"And I'm in love with you."

She laughed and hugged me closer. Her happiness was contagious. I was happier than I'd been in a long time as I held her, kissed her lips, her neck, glanced around and cursed the several beachcombers sharing the location with us.

In that moment, all my issues felt settled. The search ended here. I was where I belonged in Elaine's arms, and nothing would ever change that. What I'd dealt with these past few days only solidified that fact in my mind. She was my forever.

## CHAPTER 18:
## BLUE SUEDE SHOES

My decision, our last day on the beach, our first night at her apartment, all of it was on my mind the entire week. Derek was in Dallas following up with our phishing client, and Nikki was visiting a sick relative, so I was alone in the office with plenty of time to work out the details. By Friday, when he returned, I was ready to lay out a timeline for my relocation.

It would take at least a month to get my business in order, find a place in Wilmington, and see if I could get out of my lease here. I could keep up with our cases from both locations, Derek and I could meet regularly for teleconferences, audio-only or with video, and we could use email and texting for anything urgent. If something major happened, I could always drive in. Firms did it all the time. Besides, with the way he traveled, I was alone in the office most of the time anyway. I hoped my plans would come together easily and I could be in the same city with Elaine by Christmas. I wanted to spend every moment of that holiday with her.

When I heard him making noises down the hall, I hit the button on my office phone. "Got any plans for lunch?" I asked when he answered. I'd give him the morning to catch up before springing the news.

"Building C?" I heard his fingers clicking on the laptop keys.

"Meet you out front at noon."

As always, Derek was in a suit and tie, I was in jeans and a thin, navy sweater. November wasn't cold enough for outerwear, but as we crossed the pentagon-shaped courtyard, I could feel the change coming. A few trees still held shades of red, yellow, orange, and gold. Autumn was ending—the best time of year here. Of course, everything felt like the best to me now.

"What's on your mind?" Derek glanced over, and I noticed a different light in his blue eyes, like something had happened. I was curious, but I had to talk to him about my plans first. Saying it straight out felt like the best approach.

"I'm moving to Wilmington."

He nodded as we approached Building C. I caught the handle on the glass doors and held it as he entered.

"I expected that was coming," he said.

"But I'd like to stay on with the firm."

He didn't answer as we glanced over the menu selection. Then we each ordered the bacon club.

"While you were gone this week, I worked out the details," I continued. "It shouldn't be a problem. We can keep up by video and emails, and who knows..."

I was about to say he might be joining me before long, but I didn't want to cloud the issue. Still, with

Melissa back in her hometown, minutes away from Elaine, anything was possible.

We paid for lunch and took a seat at the stainless bar that ran around the glass outer wall. Derek didn't speak as he unwrapped the large sandwich, and I followed suit, waiting. I took a bite, and the savory tang of bacon on top of turkey and cheddar filled my mouth. As much as he and Nikki complained about this place, I'd never had a bad meal here.

After a few more bites, Derek finally responded. "I think it's a good idea."

My eyebrows rose. I'd prepared for a little debate before he caved to my expert planning. I waited for him to say more, but he didn't. The change in his expression was on my mind, and I wondered if it had anything to do with his easy concession.

"How'd it go in Dallas?" I asked, snagging a chip and popping it in my mouth. Greasy, salty, good.

He nodded, finishing another bite. "They're very happy with our work. Want us to consider handling all their online security going forward."

"Hell, yeah," I said with a smile. That corporation was worth several billion and was multi-national. We could both retire on an account like that. "I guess that's why you're onboard with whatever."

"Yeah." He lifted the soft drink he'd ordered and took a sip, and since he wasn't arguing with me, I was ready to get to the bottom of his change.

"So what happened?" I sat back.

He glanced up and then shrugged. "I just presented what we'd found, showed them all the steps we'd taken to prevent future problems—"

"I'm talking about you. You're not so... devastated anymore. If that's the right word."

He picked up a salt packet and tilted it back and forth between his fingers. I waited a few moments, wondering if he was going to tell me.

"Melissa's back in Wilmington," he said.

I remembered my encounter with her last week. She looked really good when we'd talked — worried that I had Derek with me, but good. Confident. The dark suit and professional demeanor helped. She wasn't the timid little kitten she'd been in Scottsdale. Studying the massive guy in front of me, I couldn't help but shake my head at the hold she had on him. She was tiny, but she was powerful.

"Right," I finally said. "Maybe one day we can relocate the entire office."

His dark brows lifted slightly, and he shook his head. "I don't know."

I couldn't resist. The anticipation of moving, of being so close to Elaine, had me wanting to brighten everyone's day. "She'll come around. Elaine says she still has feelings for you. It's just a matter of time."

His blue eyes snapped to me then. "Watch what you say to Elaine. I'm pretty sure Melissa doesn't like being told what to do."

That made me laugh. "No, she does *not*. Which should make you her perfect match."

He stood and took a few bills from his pocket. "I don't need good intentions backfiring."

I followed suit, clearing out so the busboys could prep for the next round of customers. Outside, the breeze had picked up, and it was starting to look like rain. I wished Elaine and I were spending the weekend together, but she had a teaching workshop all day Saturday. And I figured I'd get started on the relocation process.

Derek was quiet as we approached our building. I still wasn't satisfied with the answer he'd given me, why he was so changed. "So Melissa in Wilmington is the only reason you're better?"

"I've been watching Sloan Reynolds," he said. "Their divorce is going through, and his behavior is growing more erratic. It won't be long before he steps out of line again, and I'm going to nail him."

"And Melissa will forgive you."

He exhaled heavily as the doors opened. "I hope it'll show her how much she means to me" The hint of sadness was back.

"How do you know that guy again?" We waited for the elevators and he looked down.

"When I taught at Princeton, they had this volunteer program. He showed me the ropes — where everything was. They called it mentoring, but it was really just an orientation."

"So you weren't friends?" We were outside the office, and I felt like I understood their connection better.

"I don't know," he continued. "We went for drinks a few times. I told him about my business, offered to do a free analysis of his family's networks."

"Yeah, but that's just run-of-the mill marketing."

He nodded. "When he emailed me... I would never have thought to investigate *him* before agreeing to track Melissa." It sounded like an argument he'd told himself before. "He was worried his wife was having an affair. It seemed so cut and dried."

I patted him on the back as we entered the glass doors. "It's going to work out," I said. "Let me know if I can help. I'll do whatever I can."

"Thanks."

* * *

My phone was vibrating as I walked up to my apartment. Seeing Elaine's name on the face made me smile.

*Where are you?* her text said.

*Just getting home,* I typed back. *Wish you were here.*

The air had grown thicker since lunch, and I could taste the pending rain. Damn. Nothing would be sweeter than spending a long, stormy weekend wrapped in Elaine's arms. Another buzz. I paused when I saw Kenny's name flashing on the screen, and at the same time I remembered Elaine still thought Kenny was a guy. I needed to clear that up next time we were together.

*Hello – you alive? Hot weekend plans?* I couldn't help a smile. I'd give her a call later and catch her up. Way too much had happened for texting.

*Solo weekend,* I wrote back. *Lots to do and tell you.*

*Ditto,* she replied.

I was just lowering the phone when two cool hands covered my eyes. "Whoa!" I reached up to catch them, but the owner jumped around in front of me in a glint of green and golden blonde.

Elaine's arms were around my neck and her mouth pressed to mine before I could say another word. Warmth flooded my chest, and I quickly shoved the phone in my back pocket and pulled her to me, pressing her back against the door as our mouths opened, tongues entwining.

"What are you doing here?" I breathed, breaking our kiss just long enough to unlock my apartment.

"Are you surprised?" Her lips were right at my ear, and her breath tickled my skin before she kissed me, sending her soft, almost-rose scent all around me.

"Yes." Surprised and all kinds of awake from my head to my toes. I pushed the door closed and lifted her off the floor, my hands cupping her ass. "And now I'm horny as hell."

She laughed, wrapping her legs around my waist. Her nose wrinkled with her smile. "I don't really have a school workshop. I called a sub and drove all day so I could do this." She held my face as she peppered kisses over my cheeks, my nose, my lips. Everything she did was burning me up. "Surprise!"

"Let me help you get it exactly right," I said, carrying her straight to the bedroom.

She laughed again, and our bodies never lost contact as we slid back onto my bed. My hands fumbled down to the edge of her skirt and then under it. I curled a finger around the string of her thong and pulled it aside. She exhaled a moan, and the sound was like electricity straight to my cock. I was hard as flint and ready to be deep inside her.

"Damn, girl, you're already wet." My mouth was against her neck and her fingers were quickly undoing the buttons on her blouse.

"I've been thinking about you," she said. "And how you'll like this…"

Her shirt was open and she swept it back. My brow collapsed at the sight of a hot-red, lacy bra barely covering her breasts. "Fuck me," I groaned.

"That's exactly why I got it." She gave me that naughty smile I loved.

"Thank you," I said, kissing the soft peaks, pushed up and together in perfect mounds. I could just see the dark tops of her nipples peeking above the shallow cups, and it took all my strength not to lose it, to go slow, keep her with me.

A little noise came from her throat as my tongue slid around one of the pink buds, and her fingers were at my waist, quickly unfastening my pants. My hand hadn't left her clit, massaging softly but firmly with my thumb, while my fingers slid in and out of her. Her hips faintly rocked with my movements, and it was all fucking hot as hell. But my thoughts scrambled when her hand wrapped around my cock and started stroking, moving quickly up and down.

Mouths back together, my groan was lost in her kiss, in her soft lips pushing mine apart as our tongues met. I felt her hand getting slicker as it moved up and down my dick. I was starting to come, and my hips flexed as I held it back, trying to think of something other than her gorgeous body, her perfect tits, her lips covering mine.

"I've got to suit up," I said, kissing her again as I reached for the bedside drawer. "It's been too long since we've been here."

Her lids were lowered as she reached around to unfasten that amazing bra.

"I really like that one," I said, moving back to catch a now-free nipple in my mouth.

She caught my face, drawing me up to her. "I'm ready," she whispered. "I need you inside me."

I was pretty confident I'd never get tired of hearing her say that to me, all hot and bothered, and I was already slick as I rolled the condom on quickly. I pushed into her, and now our hips were rocking fast. She rolled us onto my back and sat up, her palms flat against the wall above my head. The tips of her breasts swayed just at my lips, and I thrust hard into her as I sat up to catch one gently between my teeth.

"Oh, god, yes!" In that moment, she let out the most amazing groan and I felt her insides tighten around my dick, pulling me right over the edge with her as her hips bucked faster, sending me deeper inside her.

I sat up and caught her ass, moving her up and down on me. Her luscious groans the greatest sound in my ears, and I closed my eyes, riding the blinding waves of my orgasm as I went off again and again inside her.

Moments later, we were collapsing, weak and sweaty, smiling and kissing each other. I was pretty certain life couldn't get any better.

"I'm having second-thoughts about relocating," I teased, pulling her close against my chest.

"You'd better not." Her slim fingers tightened in a pinch on my waist, making me laugh.

"I'm just saying. I don't want to miss any surprises."

She rose up to kiss my lips again, her soft hair spilling around us. It was messy now, a little more bedhead, a little stringy. I loved it.

"I'll find other ways to surprise you," she said with a grin. "Don't worry."

Memories of our last night in Scottsdale crossed my mind. "I believe you," I said before kissing her neck. "You are definitely the queen of surprises."

A pleased sigh came from her throat as she slid back down, her arms still around my neck.

"Maybe I'll surprise you next," I said, running my hands down the length of her back, massaging her curves, loving the feel of her body in my arms.

Her head popped up then, green eyes lit. "What did you have in mind?"

I couldn't help but laugh as my mind started ticking through the possibilities. I hadn't prepared for anything, but I had an idea. "Close your eyes," I said.

She made a big show of obeying me, and I smiled, moving her slim body to the side and getting up.

Condom pitched in the trash, I went to my closet and flipped on the light, looking around. I wasn't sure what I was going to do, but a blindfold seemed like a good start.

All I had were ties, so I picked a green one. Then my eyes fell on the gold one I'd had with me in Scottsdale. It was misshapen and nearly torn, and the memory of me struggling against it had all the blood surging below my waist again. I shook my head and exited.

Returning to the bed, I paused a moment to admire my gorgeous lady, totally nude, lying on her side waiting for me. I leaned down and kissed a breast, which caused her to let out a little yelp.

"You're such a breast man," she giggled.

"And yours are perfect." Sitting beside her, "Keep those eyes closed," I ordered. She nodded, and I pulled her arms, bringing her to a sitting position. Then I moved around and wrapped the green tie over her eyes, securing it at the back of her head.

"Hmm…" was all she said as a smile curled her lips. "What now?"

I lay her back, moving all the sheets away, staying as silent as possible. Her toenails were painted bright red, and I stopped at one slim foot, running the tip of my finger down her arch and then kissing the side of it.

"Mmm," she moaned, rubbing her knees together and reaching for me. I caught her hands and put them back at her sides.

"These stay here," I ordered. She let out another little laugh, and I smiled, trying to think of how to surprise her next.

My eyes traveled up her smooth legs, stopping where they came together. Then, with the pinky finger of my left hand, I lightly traced the line down the center of those lips, just above her clit. "I like that you keep this bare."

"Ooh, Patrick," she gasped, and her hands went to my arm.

"Hmm," I said, catching those rebellious limbs. "I have another idea," I said, standing and going back to the closet.

"Patrick?" she called, but I wasn't gone long.

I scooped the gold tie off the hanger and went back to the bed. Next I pulled her wrists to me, using one end of the tie to secure them together and the other end to hold them above her head.

"What are you doing?" Her voice was stunned as I tied her to the bronze headboard. She was unable to move now, and the sight of her that way, arms over her head, breasts pressed together, sent the blood rushing to my dick.

My brow lined at my unexpected response, and I leaned over her, speaking right next to her ear. "You really push me outside my comfort zone." My voice was low and breathy, and I was going for slightly ominous.

"Is that good?" Her head tilted to the side, and I saw her brow line.

"It's surprisingly good." I was still right at her ear. "Do you like it?"

"I don't know." Her voice had the slightest tremor in it, and I hesitated... But the memory of how much she enjoyed tying me to the chair kept me going.

"Can you get away?" I continued, taking one of her nipples between my fingers and rolling it back and forth. She moaned and strained against the tie, her knees rubbing together again. My dick was growing harder at the sight.

"No," she whispered, pulling against the gold tie.

"So you're my captive now." My hand returned to the slit just above her clit, and I dipped my pinky between her folds. Very wet.

"Ooo," she moaned, rotating her hips and pulling her wrists again. I leaned forward and kissed her mouth roughly, but pulled away when she tried to kiss me back.

"You'll do what I say," I said, in that low voice.

A little tremble moved through her body. "I don't know."

She strained against the tie again, and her breasts peaking together making my erection ache. I slid my finger deeper into the folds between her legs where it was hotter.

She shivered again, moaning. "I don't like being tied up."

Her voice was a breathy whine, and I smiled, kissing the side of her neck, working my way down to her shoulders, lower to her breasts. My two longest fingers plunged all the way inside her now, massaging what was swollen and wet. I wanted to replace those fingers with my cock, but I was toying with her the way she'd done me.

"I think you do like it." My mouth returned to her body, I kissed her, sliding my tongue down the center of her stomach.

"I want to be untied," she said, her voice a little more strained. "Please, Patrick."

"Please what?" I whispered, kissing her navel then tonguing it lightly.

"Please untie me," she gasped.

I paused then. My lips hovered just above her skin, and my brow pulled together. Her expression seemed anxious, but her body, at least judging by what I felt, was into it. I leaned up and swirled my tongue around her nipple. She let out another little whimper, and I realized, we'd just made love. What I was feeling could be residual...

Quickly I flew to the headboard and jerked the gold tie loose, then I snatched the green blindfold off her eyes, pulling her up to me and wrapping my arms tightly around her.

"Are you okay?" I whispered, kissing her cheek, her lips.

She leaned back to face me, eyes round. I wasn't sure what she was about to do. My throat tightened. Would she cry? Would she be angry?

"Why did you stop?" she said, voice high. "I was just playing along."

"What?" My shoulders dropped.

"I was being your captive, begging to be set free..."

I frowned, but the side of her mouth twitched. "You were worried?" The twitch was turning to a tiny grin as she placed her hands on my cheeks. I was getting pissed. "I'm sorry."

"Dammit, Elaine." I started to get up, releasing her altogether. But she was on me, grabbing me fast by the shoulders.

"Don't be mad!" she cried.

I stood at the bedside, and she was on her knees, holding me, her face struggling between laughter and worry.

I exhaled deeply. "You have no idea how it goes against all my instincts to hear you beg me to stop and ignore it."

She rested her head on my shoulder still holding her arms tight around my neck. "I love you so much."

It was impossible to stay mad when she said that. I wrapped my arms around her waist and gave in completely, pulling her close.

Her head popped up then, that glimmer back in her eyes. "This is why we need a safe word."

"Motherfu—," my hands went back to her waist, but she shook my shoulders.

"I'm serious! Then we know for sure if one of us needs to stop."

"A safe word."

"Something you'd never say during sex."

"Like what?" I was sure my expression was as skeptical as I felt because her eyebrow arched like she was fixing to tease me.

"Bubblegum."

"What?"

"Yes!" She hopped off the bed and picked up the gold tie. "Wow. You really messed this one up."

I took it from her and went into the closet, hanging it back on the peg. "One of my hundred-dollar ties, no less."

She was right behind me, slipping those cool, slim hands around my waist. Her bare breasts pressed against my back as her fingers spread out over my stomach. I took one of her hands and lifted it to my lips. My erection had only cooled a little.

"So *bubblegum*," I repeated, walking out of the closet and pulling her with me.

"Yes," she hopped on the bed again. "If one of us is going too far or if it hurts too much—"

"I don't like the sound of that."

"Say *bubblegum* and it stops," she continued unfazed. "That's the deal."

"It's like a magic word," I said, curling a blonde strand around my finger.

She tilted her chin up, shaking her pretty head. "No, the magic word is *please*. The safe word is *bubblegum*." Then she laughed and kissed me.

"I think we need to test this." My hands had just gone to her cheeks, cupping her face when I noticed a loud tapping noise from the other room.

Our lips stilled and I raised my head. We exchanged a confused look, but I let her go, picking up my jeans and jerking them over my hips.

"Hold that thought, Bubblegum," I said.

"You can't use it all the time or it won't work!"

I shook my head as the tapping grew louder and went to the door. "Hang on," I called, pulling it open fast. The girl outside my door jumped back.

"Oh!" she said, and for a half-second, I didn't recognize her. Light-brown, shoulder-length hair. Her lips were a rosy pink, and she only wore the lightest mascara. It was smudged a bit under big blue eyes. She was the same, but completely different.

"Kenny?"

Those eyes flew down my shirtless torso and back up as her cheeks flooded with pink. "This is how you answer the door?" she exhaled, shaking her head as she pushed past me, entering my apartment.

"What are you doing here?" I followed her back inside, shutting it.

She went to the fireplace and stood staring at the silent space while I took in her short dress with black combat boots. The edge wasn't completely gone.

"I've been needing to talk to you, but you've been away so much." She turned to face me, wringing her small hands. "When you texted that you were alone this weekend, I figured I'd just drive up and spend the night."

My brow lined and I shook my head. "What's going on?"

"Oh, Patrick." Those hands went to her forehead, and she pushed back her now-even hair. It was a gesture I recognized from the tattoo parlor when she'd forgotten to get my signature on the paperwork. Her eyes rose to mine, and now they were shining with tears.

"Hey," I crossed the room quickly to hug her. "What's wrong?" I rubbed her back, holding her close. "Did your parents kick you out?"

"No," her voice trembled. "But they might. Oh, god."

Her hands went to my arms and she pushed out of them. Then she took another step away, and her eyes scanned my body again.

"Why aren't you wearing a shirt?" she said, her voice irritated. "It's hard to think when you're all… on display like this."

"Jesus, will you just tell me what's going on?"

With a deep inhale, she straightened her back. Then closing her eyes, she said it. The two words that exploded everything.

"I'm pregnant."

## CHAPTER 19:
## RIGHT AND WRONG

It felt like a roundhouse kick to the gut followed by an ice-chest of freezing water dumped over my head, but I still wasn't ready to accept Kenny's meaning. "Why are you telling me you're pregnant?"

"Because it's yours, dummy!" Her hands slapped down to her legs and she stormed into the kitchen, jerking open my refrigerator as she spoke under her breath. "What I wouldn't give for a drink right now."

I was right behind her. "But... You were on the pill."

"Yes." She took out a ginger ale and popped the top. "All I can figure is I'd had a sinus infection the week before. The doc put me on antibiotics—"

"Kenny, what the hell?" I leaned back against the bar. Now I was the one shoving my hands into my hair.

"Don't raise your voice at me, Patrick Knight!" She flashed, and I took one glance before grabbing the reins on my freaking-out insides. I was ready to yell, but not at Ken.

Instead, I opened the cabinet and pulled down the Jack and two shot glasses. I filled both to the rim with amber liquid as she watched me.

"I can't drink right now."

Without a word, I lifted one and shot it followed quickly by the second, wincing at the burn. "Shit."

"Yeah." Her voice was hesitant. "That's what I expected you to say."

Clearing my throat, I felt only slightly more ready for this. At least my tone was calmer. "So you were taking antibiotics?"

Her shoulders relaxed. "I'd been off them a few days. Honestly, I forgot all about it. You might remember we weren't thinking so clearly that night."

I remembered everything about that night—down to her crying in my arms at the end. "And you're sure it's mine?"

She leaned forward and punched my chest hard. "You think I'd lie to you? You're the only guy I've slept with since Blake."

Rubbing the spot where she'd hit me, I tried to process this. My stomach was in knots; my emotions were flying all over the place. On the one hand, I wasn't pissed that Kenny was having a little baby, but *Jesus H. Christ!* It wasn't supposed to be mine.

"I don't know what to say." I finally admitted. "I mean, we're not really together. Did you want me to pro—"

"Stop." She held up a hand. "Just stop right there. I didn't come here for you to make some grand gesture." Shaking her head, she tried to leave the kitchen, but I caught her. "That's not how we are, Patrick."

Her blue eyes held mine, and I knew she was right. The thought of me getting down on my knee to her was followed closely by the image of her bursting out laughing. But I wouldn't walk away from this, I wouldn't walk away from her. *Dammit*, I had no idea what she needed from me, but I'd give it to her.

"I want to help you, Ken."

"Then be my friend. Just... be there for me."

My grip on her arm loosened, and I pulled her to my chest. "I'm always that, babe."

I held her close, but a soft voice from the living room snapped everything back to the present.

"Patrick?" It was Elaine, standing in the doorway, dressed now in her skirt and my shirt. "What's going on?"

I crossed the room to her, all of my insides tight. "Elaine, this is Kenny."

Elaine's brow rose, and my stomach dropped. "Kenny's a girl?"

I felt my guest approaching from behind. "You said you were alone this weekend—" Kenny started.

"Yes." My eyes hadn't left Elaine's, and I saw the hurt growing there. *Shit shit shit...* "I was going to tell you about the mixup, but we got distracted and—"

"You told her you were going to be alone this weekend, so she came here to spend the night with you? And she's pregnant?"

That's when it all went to hell. Elaine's green eyes glistened as they moved from me to the girl standing behind me.

"It's not like that."

"I didn't know," Kenny said.

"Oh my god, Patrick!" Elaine quickly moved around the room, collecting her shoes and her bag, but I was with her every step of the way.

"Wait," I said as she pushed past me. Her face was crumbling, and all my insides were crumbling with it. "Baby—"

"Don't you dare." Her voice was quiet, but sharp. She sniffed, and my own eyes grew damp.

I caught her waist, stopping her as she tried to walk out my door. "Please. You can't drive back to Wilmington like this."

She wouldn't look at me. "I'm not. I'll get a room for the night."

"Stay with me… I can explain."

She only pushed my arms away and dashed out the door. I followed, but she wouldn't stop. She was down the stairs and at her car without looking back. I stood on the sidewalk as the first drops of rain started to fall, watching as her tail lights disappeared around the corner.

* * *

My heart was through the floor. Kenny was beside me on the couch as I sat like a zombie, sending what felt like the five thousandth text message to Elaine. They all said the same things, *I'm sorry. I love you. Please talk to me. It's not what you think. We can figure this out.*

I'd given up calling when I'd gotten her voice mail for the fifth time.

"I'm so sorry, Patrick." Kenny's voice was quiet as she watched me type. "I thought you were alone."

Pressing my lips together, I put the phone down but against my leg in case it vibrated. "It's not your fault. Elaine surprised me tonight." The memory, that red bra, was another twist to the knife in my insides.

"I should've told you I was coming. I just—"

"Forget it. Let's talk about this," I said. My throat was tight, everything was tight, but we had some major decision-making ahead of us. "What do you want to do?"

She sat back then, crossing her legs in front of her as she faced me. "I'm thinking a hundred things at once," she sighed. "I can't do this alone, but we're not a couple. I can't tell my parents, but they're going to find out eventually. I can't afford my own place..." Then her head dropped into her hands, and her voice broke. "Oh, god, what makes me think I can have a baby if I can't even afford my own place?"

Tears hit her cheeks, and that old protectiveness I had for her resurfaced. "Stop." I pulled her to me, rubbing her back. "It doesn't matter that we're not a couple. I'm still here. I can help you get a place or whatever you need."

"I'm sorry, I've been trying not to cry," she sniffed, sitting back, and wiping her eyes with the back of her hands. Now I understood why her mascara was smudged. "Fucking tequila. I can't believe I'm pregnant. God, Patrick, I feel like... such an idiot high schooler."

"We'll figure it out," I said, pulling her hands into my lap and rubbing them. "Tell me what you want to do. Do you want to keep it?"

Her lips tightened and for a moment she sat quietly holding my hands. Then her blue eyes rose to mine, and she nodded as my phone buzzed beside me.

"Okay, we'll start there," I said. My eyes went to the phone, and the name that had been circling through my mind for the last hour appeared. Elaine. "Hang on."

Scooping it up, I ran back to my bedroom. "Elaine?"

"I only called because you won't stop texting." Her voice was soft, but I could tell she'd been crying. My chest ached, and I wanted to find her, bring her back to me, hold her until she saw this didn't change anything between us. Nothing could change how I felt about her.

"I'm so glad you did," I said. "We've got to talk this out."

"I can't help feeling like you lied to me. About a lot of things."

I shook my head, but she couldn't see me. "It wasn't like that. When you said that, when I realized your mistake, I wasn't really thinking about Kenny being a girl or how it looked…"

"It looks like you slept with her," she said, and my stomach ached.

"I did, but—"

"And she texts you all the time. You're obviously very close," I heard her breath catch. "And now she's having your baby?"

"None of that changes how I feel about you."

"This is why long distance doesn't work. I can't do this, Patrick."

Her words cut through me, and everything in me rejected what she was saying. "No. Elaine, please." My voice was breaking now, along with my heart.

"I need a break. You need to deal with… what's happening. I'll call you when I'm ready to talk."

"Elaine—" but she'd ended the call.

The line was silent, and my head dropped. I lay back on the bed, pressing my palms against my eyes. Pain hit me again and again like a sledgehammer to the chest, and all I could think of was Elaine, her beautiful smile, her touch. I'd lost her again, but this time it was my fault. And I was pretty sure she wouldn't be back in a week. My insides clenched so hard, my knees bent, and I rolled onto my side, pressing my face into the pillow. It still smelled like her. *Jesus.*

I felt the lightest touch on my shoulder and blinked back. Worried blue eyes watched me.

"Hey," I rolled over and sat up, temporarily forgetting the pain hammering my insides. I had to take care of what was happening here. Elaine was right about that at least.

Kenny hesitated, then she lifted her hand and touched my cheek with the backs of her slim fingers. "Are you crying?"

Quickly, I shoved any moisture away. "It's not about you. Or the baby."

Her dark brow pierced, and I could tell she didn't believe me. "Bee sting or needle?"

My phone dropped out of my hand, as I covered my eyes against the warm mist. "You were right." My voice was thick. "Nothing hurts as bad as this."

She leaned forward and hugged me. "Nothing kicks the shit out of you like love."

I held her back, speaking into her hair. "And I really fucking love her."

She pulled away and studied my face a moment then cupped it in her hands, wiping her thumbs under my eyes. The memory of us in the back of my car, me doing the same thing to her crossed my mind. "Then we're really fucking going to get her back."

Shaking my head, I took her hands and brought them down to my lap. "She thought you were a guy."

"Why did you let her think that?"

"I didn't mean to… It's hard to explain." Exhaling heavily, I moved to sit against the headboard, pushing the pillows up behind me. She crawled up next to me and rested her head on my chest. Slim arms went around my waist, my arm was over her shoulder. "How are you feeling?" I said.

She shrugged. "Exhausted. All the time."

Holding her like this, thinking about Elaine's words, I was at a total loss. This situation had sent everything into a tailspin. If Kenny had my baby, we'd be bonded in a way — a way I wasn't sure how to interpret. I did care about this tiny woman, but not as my wife. Elaine's face was all over that category in my heart.

"I have to tell you the truth," I said quietly. "This is kind of blowing my mind a little."

"How do you think I feel?" she sighed. "I've been thinking about it nonstop for two weeks. That's why I finally came here. I knew you could help me figure it out. I'm just sorry I messed up everything for you."

My grip tightened on her shoulder. "I'll work that out. You said you want to keep the baby, but what does that mean? Do you need money? Do you need me to help you find a place?"

Her shoulder went up and down. "I don't know. I probably should tell my parents."

"Okay," I nodded. "I'll go with you to do that."

"Thanks," she said.

The sky flashed briefly, and a roll of thunder vibrated the windows. Kenny's arm tightened over my waist, and I rubbed her slim shoulder.

"I'm really tired now," she said.

I was comfortable enough, and I was pretty sure I'd be awake all night anyway. "Sleep," I said. "I'll take care of you. Don't worry about anything."

"Thanks, Patrick," she said, and I could hear her voice growing distant. "One thing's for sure. It'll be a beautiful baby."

My throat tightened as the noise of the rain grew louder. Kenny fell asleep quickly, and I held her, my brain cycling through everything that just happened. Thunder rumbled, and all I could think of was Elaine out there somewhere, alone in this storm thinking who knew what.

Memories of walking on the beach with her, of her mentioning the little student and thinking about my babies... pain clenched my chest again, and I picked up my phone. One more time, I had to be sure she knew. I texted, *I love you.*

\* \* \*

Kenny's parents were not what I expected.

After a night of small doses of sleep marked by tossing and turning—while Kenny slept like a rock curled up beside me—I'd finally given up. I'd cooked eggs for both of us for breakfast, and she ate half of my portion in addition to hers. Then I put on my most respectable-looking khakis and a button down, and we hit the road for Bayville, me following her in my car.

In a little more than an hour, Kenny and I were sitting side by side on a dark plaid sofa in the living room of a small, middle-class home with pictures of Kenny at various ages on wood-paneled walls.

Her father Byron Woods had light brown hair like his daughter's that was now becoming salt-and-pepper grey. He studied me with stern suspicion from his chair, which I didn't necessarily fault him for.

Kenny's mother Grace hastened around the room getting everyone drinks. Other than her dark hair, Kenny looked more like Grace, having the same build and eye color. I wasn't sure what she was expecting or if she already had an idea.

"What's your line of work Mr. Knight?" Kenny's dad asked, sitting back in his recliner with a glass of iced tea.

Kenny was right, this did feel exactly like we were in high school confessing. "I'm a private investigator, sir. I can do pretty much anything, but my focus is online security."

The part about me being a closer and getting the job done didn't seem quite appropriate in view of our circumstances.

"How did you and Kenny meet?" her mom breezed into the room, carrying another glass of tea, which she handed to me.

That question threw me. I didn't know how Kenny's parents felt about her former occupation—if she'd even told them about her job with Carl or being a tattoo artist. They appeared pretty conservative. Then I remembered how Kenny looked when we first met compared to how she looked today. The change had occurred since she moved back home, all her tattoos were hidden; I was stumped.

"Patrick works with Derek Alexander. The man who helped with Blake's case?" Ken intercepted. "We met through mutual friends."

Both her parents nodded, and we were all quiet again. For the first time since Kenny told me, I worried what other people might think about our situation. I thought of my sister Amy, and how I would feel if a guy showed up to drop a bomb like this. I'd punch him in the face. How could I say this gently?

"We've had a little surprise," I started, shifting in my seat. "You see—"

"Mom, Dad," Kenny cut in, "I'm pregnant."

With a gasp, Kenny's mom covered her heart with her hand. Then she let out an "Oh!" that I was pretty sure indicated she was *not* devastated by the news.

"And you're the father?" Kenny's dad was another matter. His eyes were no longer curious. They were flat.

"Yes, sir." I shifted. I should probably *let* him punch me in the face if he wanted to, only he wasn't that big. "I… I mean, *we*…"

"It was an accident," Kenny said. "We didn't mean for it to happen. It was just one of those things where—"

"Kendra," her mother said softly. "You don't have to tell us everything."

Somehow that statement made me want to laugh. No, her mother probably didn't want to know the whole story of how this blessed event occurred.

Her father sat forward. "So why are we all here? Do you have a plan?"

"Yes, Patrick's staying in Princeton, and I want to stay here with you in Bayville." Kenny sounded more confident than she had in two days. I hoped it was because I was here with her, and I sat back to let her take the lead. Whatever she said, I'd support it.

"If it's okay with you," she continued, "I'll keep working at the Jungle Gym until I can afford my own place."

My brow lined. I hadn't asked her what she was doing these days, and with a name like that, I wasn't sure if she was working with kids, animals, or exercisers.

"How will you do that?" her mother asked. "You can't kickbox in your condition."

"Sure I can!" She scooted forward on the couch. "And I'd like to keep going to GCU, finish my teaching certificate…"

213

All of this was news to me, but it was great. She was doing a lot more than she'd told me.

"I'll help out any way I can," I added.

Her father looked at me a moment, and then he stood. "So you're not planning to get married?"

"No." Kenny answered before I could speak. "Patrick's... Neither of us intended to be together that way."

"I'm not happy about this, Kendra." His voice was stern.

I stood as well at that. "I do care about your daughter, sir." I walked over to him, then I wished I hadn't. I was a bit taller, and I wasn't going for intimidation. "This is my responsibility, too."

"You're damn right it is. I expect to hear a plan that demonstrates how Kendra can actually afford her own place and a baby while she works and goes to school. To me it sounds more like another screw-up that will land her right back here. For good."

His word choice pissed me off, but his point was one I'd been going over in my own head all night—when I wasn't thinking about Elaine. "I make good money, sir. I'm in a position to help Kenny with whatever—"

"We're still working out the details, Dad."

While I was going for diplomacy, Kenny's sharp tone sounded ready to fight. I was pretty sure that was *not* the best approach, and I wished we'd planned this out before driving here. Thankfully her mother intervened.

"Byron, it sounds like they're working on a plan. We can give them a little time." Then she turned to her daughter. "When are you due, honey? You're barely showing!"

"May."

The room fell silent for what felt like a long time. I searched for something to say, but I felt like we'd said all we could to this point.

Her father walked to the small liquor cabinet and took out two tumblers. He poured a finger of scotch into each and handed me one. "I suppose congratulations are in order."

I nodded and took the drink. "Thanks. And trust me, sir. I'm going to make this right."

He turned to his daughter. "Kendra, you can stay here for now. Patrick is welcome to visit you any time, of course. But I expect you to give me a real solution. Soon."

Her brow relaxed, and she stood. "I will, Dad. I promise."

* * *

Later that night after a dinner of pork chops, lettuce wedges, mac and cheese — again with Kenny eating half of mine — I drove her down to the pier. She directed me and after a few turns, we were walking down the long wooden structure that extended over the water.

"Well, that went about how I expected," she sighed.

I reached over and took her hand. "You need to work on your delivery when asking for favors."

"Ugh! You're right. I know you're right." She shook her head. "He drives me crazy. I'm sitting there telling him my plan, and he acts like I've gone total charity case."

"Speaking of that, you said you didn't know what to do. It sounds like you have a few pretty good idea in the works."

We were at the end of the pier, and she sat. Then she tugged on my arm, making me sit beside her, our feet dangling over the edge. "I've been thinking about it a lot. I guess when I saw my dad's face, it all just clicked together."

"You've got a job, you're going to GCU... That's all great."

She exhaled a little laugh. "I just wish I could afford my own place *now*."

"I can pay for deposits or whatever. Tell me where and when, and I'll send you the money."

"No, Mom's right. It doesn't seem like the right thing yet. I'll need help with the baby—"

"I want to help you."

Her fingers traveled to the band she'd made around my arm, and I watched as she traced the lines with the tips of her fingers. "This is some of my best work."

"Removal of Long-Story Stacy," I said, remembering. We were quiet a few moments, then I took her hand and turned it over, opening it to show the tear hidden in her palm. "Did you ever want a family with him?"

Her fingers curled closed over mine, and after a few quiet moments, she shook her head. "We didn't have a chance to think about it. We were so young, and he was gone so fast."

My lips pressed together, and I smoothed her palm out against mine. "Some things stop you in your tracks."

"Yeah." Her voice was thick, and she spread her fingers so they threaded with mine. "Thanks for coming here, standing by me. I can honestly tell this baby I loved its daddy very much."

"Oh, Ken," I whispered, pulling her cheek to my chest and holding her.

My feelings toward Kenny were all twisted up. They were strong, but they moved in a different direction from my feelings for Elaine. I didn't want to be with Kenny that way, and I believed her when she said she didn't want to marry me. At the same time, she was part of my life now, and I cared about her. I loved her.

"I expect you to tell me if that little guy needs anything," I said, hoping to lighten the mood.

"Oh, so it's a boy?"

"Already causing this much trouble? Definitely."

She laughed, pushing out of my arms. It sounded good. "You're a dangerously sweet man, Bingley."

"And you've been dealt some tough cards." Reaching up, I slid her light brown hair off her cheek and met her smile. "No matter what, I'm here for you. I meant it two months ago, and I mean it now."

She nodded and took my hand from her cheek, kissing it before starting to stand, pulling me up with her. "Let's get going. I'm as settled as I can be for now, and you've got to win your lady love back."

I followed her up the pier to my car, still holding hands. "I don't know if she'll be as easy to convince as your parents."

"If she's as torn up about you as you are about her, she will."

I wasn't sure she was right, but I nodded, keeping my smile in place. "I'll probably have to give her a little time."

"If there's anything I can do, let me know." She imitated my tone.

I pinched her nose. "I will."

\* \* \*

Back in Princeton, I paced my apartment, holding the phone to my ear and trying to figure out what I could say or do that I hadn't already. I knew it was too soon to go to her, but I needed to hear her voice, to know what she was thinking. After several rings, my stomach sank. It seemed she was back to not taking my calls, but just as I was giving up, her voice appeared on the other end of the line. My eyes closed automatically at the sound.

"I don't want to talk to you yet," she said quietly.

"Okay," I answered. The fact that she said *yet* gave me the tiniest bit of hope. "I just wanted to be sure you made it home. I... You know how I feel, Elaine."

"Don't," her voice cracked, and I felt it across the miles directly to my heart.

"Nothing's changed," I said softly. "What happened with her was way before us, and it's just one of those things. An unexpected..." I didn't want to say *problem*. "Something we can deal with."

"You didn't tell me she was a girl."

"And I was wrong. I'll never keep anything like that from you again. It just didn't seem so urgent at the time."

"We're miles apart, you're communicating with a secret ex-girlfriend, and now this." Her tone was more heartbroken than attacking. I knew she was telling me all the thoughts swirling through her head, and I wanted to squash them all.

"Listen to me," I said. "My feelings aren't like that. Kenny's like a little sister to me."

"Who you sleep with."

With that one phrase, I lost.

I rested my head against the doorjamb, eyes closed. "We'd had a lot to drink, I was in a really bad place—"

"Oh, Patrick," tears were in her voice, and my chest ached at the sound. "Loving you, having you break my heart... I couldn't take that."

The frustration was driving me crazy. I wanted to go to her, wipe those tears away and love her until she believed me. "I'll never hurt you," I said.

"You already have."

"Elaine," I pleaded. "You know this doesn't change anything."

"It changes some things."

"Not how much I love you."

"I've got to go." The line went dead and my hand dropped.

For a few minutes, I struggled against slamming my phone against the wall. Her words repeated over and over in my head. She was right, but she was wrong. The news was a shock, and my life had suddenly shifted. Kenny and the baby were new priorities for me, but they didn't touch us and our relationship. She was still the most important thing. But I couldn't force her to believe it. Only time would prove it to her, and as much as it hurt, I had to wait. My jaw clenched, and I was back to pacing.

The one thing I couldn't take was the idea she might walk away. That her feelings might change because of this. She didn't say they had, but I could feel her mounting her defenses against me.

"Dammit!" I slammed my palm against the door jamb. I wasn't the enemy. I wouldn't hurt her.

She said I already had.

I placed the phone on the counter and slowly went to the shower. Flipping on the water, I watched as the steam started to rise. I wanted to hold her again. I *needed* to hold her again. My insides hurt, everything hurt as the warm water covered my face, as I stepped under the spray gutted.

# CHAPTER 20:
## THE REDEMPTION BOX

Derek didn't look up from his laptop when I entered his office the next morning.

"I need a project. Something big," I said, watching as he leaned back in his chair, blue eyes on me now, brow creased. "I need something that'll take a lot of time and mental energy."

He didn't ask questions, which I appreciated; instead he leaned forward and started typing. "I'll send you all the information on our new Dallas client. They need a complete online security diagnostic. Check every system, portal, communications channel... look for any and all vulnerable spots, write it up and detail all the fixes we recommend. Then I need you to contact Syntech and get them started integrating us into their networks. Make a list of every ID we should have access to and detail what we will and won't see, data we will and won't retain." He did a few finishing keystrokes. "That should take you a while."

I nodded, and he studied me a moment. "You okay?"

"Yes." I was already out the door. "Thanks."

* * *

Two weeks of analyzing portal after portal, working late, avoiding being alone in my apartment as much as possible, lifting weights with Derek, running, basically doing everything in my power not to think about her all the time, I was exhausted.

And I still thought about her all the time.

Thanksgiving came and went, and instead of spending the holiday with Elaine, I'd spent it alone at my apartment, eating a cold turkey sandwich, lying on my couch, and watching football.

Kenny checked in at least. "Why is the father of my child spending this family holiday alone?"

"It's okay," I lied. "My family's deal is at Christmas. We're too spread out for both holidays. Anyway, I'm not the best company right now."

"Well, we had the entire Woods clan here, and let me tell you, I would rather be hiding out with you."

Somehow Kenny could still make me smile. "How's my little troublemaker cooking?"

"As far as I can tell, just fine," she said with an exhale. It sounded like she lay back. "But something happened today... It might be a plan that would satisfy my dad, and I want to know what you think."

Sitting forward in my chair, I muted the game. "Okay, shoot."

"My aunt Laura was in town for the holiday," she paused as if choosing her words. "She's an interesting person. My mom's sister, single, but a very successful businesswoman."

She waited as if I were supposed to say something.

"That's... nice?"

"Anyway, she was talking about how she'd considered adoption before, but the paperwork and the whole process was so tedious and overwhelming..." another pause. "I want to ask her if she'd like to adopt Peanut."

Kenny said it in such a rush, it took me a moment to catch up. "Who?"

"My aunt Laura—"

"No... you're calling the baby Peanut?"

"Would you focus? She lives in New York, so she's not far from here. She's got plenty of money, and, well, it's a longshot. But at least it's family?"

Her tone was optimistic, but I needed to be sure. "Is that something you think you can do?"

"Would you be okay with it?"

I thought about that. Relief was my initial response, but I wasn't sure I could trust that emotion. Still, when it came down to it, a loving aunt who wanted a baby, who was related to Ken...

"I think, considering what's going on with both of us, where we are and what we're prepared to do, it's probably the best solution. If you think your aunt will be a good mom?"

A huge sigh filled my ear. "She'll be the best mom." I could tell Kenny was smiling now. "I always loved visiting her when I was a kid. And they'll be in New York! Imagine if the baby's an artist."

"Like you." A return-smile crossed my lips. "Ken, if it makes you this happy, I trust you. Do you need me to do anything?"

"No, that's just it. We'll work out all the details." She paused a moment, and I waited. "Thank you, Patrick."

"I don't feel like I've done enough—tell me if I can help you, okay?"

"I will," she said.

"Take care of yourself."

Kenny's optimism was contagious, and knowing we had a solution, I was brave enough to take a chance. Hopping over to my recent calls, I touched the name I loved. Waiting as it rang, I realized she was probably with family and not able to talk.

Hearing her voice in the greeting still tightened my stomach. I missed her so much. "Just thinking about you," I said in my message. "Hope you're having a nice holiday. I love you."

Leaning back in the chair again, I couldn't give up hope. I had to believe Elaine and I would be together for Christmas.

\* \* \*

Another week of getting through the hours, and by Thursday, the report for our Dallas client was done. Derek hadn't questioned my sudden, work-obsessed behavior, and I hadn't said anything to him about my relocation being on hold. Our Dallas analysis was completed in record time, and the only complaint I could imagine them having would come in the future. When they asked why our subsequent services took longer.

Time of day wasn't even on my radar when I noticed a tapping on my door. Looking up, it was already growing dark outside.

"Let's shut it down, hit the gym." Derek was in my doorway, and I looked up briefly before returning to my laptop. He was right, and I was tired.

"Sure," I said. "Be right there."

A few clicks later, I was heading out, saying goodnight to Nikki and crossing the courtyard to Building E. A quick change in the locker room, and I was joining my partner on the bench.

"I'll be out for the rest of the week," Derek said through an exhale. Our gym visits had become more sporadic in the last weeks. He was gone more and actually seemed less driven, his spotting needs less frequent.

"What's going on?" I asked, thinking how things had changed. I was the driven one now, pushing too hard, looking for any way to kill the nonstop ache grinding in my chest.

He dropped the large dumbbell on the rack and picked up a towel. "I'm not into this tonight. You feel like getting a drink?"

I finished my set and then nodded. "Sure."

* * *

The Tavern on the Corner was a new bar within walking distance of our office complex, and as such, it smelled too fresh to me. The glossy wood shone too brightly, and as it was Thursday, we saw too many familiar faces from around the offices. It wasn't the right atmosphere for the pain-killing drunk I'd had in mind when I agreed to ditch the workout for the bar, but I'd deal with it.

"So where you headed?" I asked once the server had placed my usual vodka in front of me. Derek was having a beer.

"Sloan's hiring prostitutes again," he said, lifting the curvy glass and taking a sip. "I want to see if one of them will talk to me, help me put him away."

"The fuck is wrong with that guy," I exhaled, lifting my stocky tumbler and taking a sip. "Mel's gorgeous, and with the way you've been stuck…"

I decided not to finish that sentence, but he knew what I was getting at. "He's a lot sicker than I ever knew," Derek said quietly.

We were both silent a moment, and a thought I hadn't considered lit in my brain. "I might have someone who can help you."

"With what?"

"Remember the setup? The deal you told me to forget about?"

Frowning, he studied my face. "Yeah?"

"Well, I didn't forget about it. I tracked Star down." I waited, gauging his response. So far it was neutral. "She was hired. She's a professional."

"Who hired her?"

"The who and the why part is stupid. I've dealt with it. But I was thinking, Star might work with you if I asked her."

He was quiet, but I could tell he was thinking about what I said. "What makes you think she'd do it?"

I shrugged. "I'd just say she's helping us get an abusive asshole behind bars. She seems like the type that would matter to."

He nodded slightly. "Hold that thought," he said. "Let me see how it goes tomorrow, then maybe."

The bartender served me a second vodka, and I took a sip. Maybe my reckless behavior could help someone. At least it might give me one point in the redemption box.

"Speaking of stuck," Derek studied me. "When are you going to tell me what happened?"

The drink was making my insides feel less achy. The edge of the pain I'd been wrestling too long was dulling. Maybe it was time to share.

I muttered into my glass before taking a longer hit. "Elaine's... I don't know. She's not talking to me."

"With how you two were? What the hell did you do?"

My lips curled into a frown, and I squinted as I said it. "I got Kenny pregnant."

From my peripheral vision, I could see Derek's brow shoot up. "Did you just say —"

"Yes," I exhaled. "It was way before, back when I was being stupid. She was on antibiotics or something and, well..."

He didn't say anything. Instead, he turned back to the bar and looked at his drink a moment. "By Kenny, you mean the little girl who works with Carl?"

"That's the one." I felt like an ass.

"She's young. What are you going to do about it?"

"I already did it. I went with her to tell her parents. She has a relative who wants to adopt the baby. I told her I'd do anything she needs." Rubbing my forehead hard, I tried again for a pain-relieving exhale. "I just don't know what to do about Elaine, to show her nothing matters to me as much as she does."

"Go to her," he said flatly.

"What?" I dropped my arm and looked at him.

"Go to her. Beg her to forgive you. Grovel if you have to."

Shaking my head. "You're one to talk. You haven't been near Melissa since—"

"It's a completely different situation. Melissa thinks I knew about what was happening to her. She thinks I helped the guy who hurt her. I'm trying to prove I didn't, and I'll do whatever it takes to nail him. You've already done everything. Go and tell her."

My brow lined. "I don't know. She was pretty upset."

"It's been two weeks?"

"Almost three."

He nodded. "Do what you want. I'm just saying what I'd do."

For a moment, I only stared ahead thinking. My drink was finished, so I slipped off the stool. The too-bright bar with its too-bright wood that smelled of too-fresh varnish was getting to me.

"I'll think about it," I said. "Have a good trip."

In the cab headed home, I did think about Derek's advice. The more I considered it, the more it made sense to me. Back at my apartment, I pulled out a case and threw some clothes inside. In the morning I'd get on the road to Wilmington.

## CHAPTER 21:
### BUBBLEGUM

Finding her, being with her, holding her in my arms—the images burned hot in my brain the entire drive south. Three weeks of waiting, of wishing I could change things, of trying to find anything to fix it, had me wound so tightly, I almost couldn't take it anymore. The miles felt like they spread out longer the closer I got to her, and I wanted to pull the car over and run the rest of the way, which didn't make sense. The Charger was much faster.

When I finally reached the school, it was dark. For a moment I sat there contemplating what I was about to do. Her last words to me tried to creep into my brain, but I forcefully shoved them out. That was three weeks ago, a lifetime it felt like, and before I'd let any second-thoughts kick in, I turned the wheel and pushed the pedal down. I was at her condo in less than five, my body humming as I sat out in front of her place. If she asked me to leave, I'd leave, but I wasn't losing another day wondering.

My knock on her door seemed too loud to me, but anticipation had all my senses heightened. We hadn't spoken, she hadn't returned my calls. This was crazy. I was crazy. My head was spinning when the door opened quickly, and Elaine appeared. She was so beautiful, I almost couldn't breathe at the sight of her.

"Patrick!" Her mouth dropped open, but I didn't wait. I rushed forward and pulled her to me, burying my face in her hair.

"I'm sorry," I whispered, fighting to keep my voice even as adrenaline flooded my veins. "I couldn't go another day without telling you in person."

Her arms fluttered up, and she rested her hands on my shoulders. I took it as an encouraging sign. "Patrick," she said again, but I wasn't done.

"I know you asked for time, and I've done my best to stay away." I was still holding her close, my lips at her ear. "I need to tell you this, and if you still want me to go, I'll go."

I stepped back then, meeting her eyes. She blinked rapidly, and I wasn't sure if tears were a good or bad sign.

"You drove here from Princeton?" she asked, and I nodded. Then she nodded as well. "Come inside and tell me."

The tiniest flicker of hope sparked in my chest. She was letting me in.

"Before I met you, Elaine, I was out of control. I'd been hurt and I was angry and I didn't believe in love anymore. I'd decided anyone who'd commit themselves to another person was a… fucking loser."

She didn't take her eyes from mine, and for a moment, I couldn't believe I'd ever doubted I could feel this way about another person again. "And then I met you, and in one night, you changed everything."

Her chin dropped, but I stepped forward, catching it and lifting her eyes to mine. She didn't struggle, and gazing into her beautiful green eyes, my heart ached with all I needed her to know.

"Everything that was wrong with me, all the pieces that were broken or that I'd tried to force into the wrong spots were fixed. Your smile, your touch... everything about you made me want to be a better person. You put me back together, Elaine, and not just that, you're beautiful and sexy... You're the only woman I want. You're the only person who completes me. None of this other stuff matters, nothing matters to me as much as you do." My voice was a cracked whisper. "Nothing."

She shook her head, eyes glistening, but I leaned down and kissed her. She didn't pull away, and I drew her closer, wrapping my arms around her, my chest rising with every movement of my lips against hers.

Then I felt the pressure of her hands on my arms. She was pushing me back.

Releasing her, my heartbeat, my breath stilled, waiting. Would she ask me to leave? The mere suggestion shot pain through my core.

"I don't know, Patrick." I could tell she was trying not to cry. "It hurts so much." Her head dropped, and a tear fell. My insides twisted. "I wanted..."

A few seconds passed, and she didn't finish.

"What did you want?"

She sniffed and for a moment she didn't speak. When at last she did, her voice was barely above a whisper. "I wanted to be the one having your baby."

"What?" I swept her back into my arms, and though she tried to push away, I held her tight until she gave in, staying in my embrace, close to my heart. "I want you to have my baby. When you're ready, I mean."

She shook her head, but I could tell she was weakening. I took a chance and leaned in for another kiss. She gave me a small kiss back before turning her cheek, and I had to fight everything in me that wanted to take her face in my hands and kiss her over and over, to make up for every day I'd missed.

"Are there any more secrets you're keeping from me?" she said, still resistant. "Any more men who are really women just waiting to surprise us?"

"God, I hope not." My forehead rested on hers, my hope rising again.

"I'm serious."

My arms did relax at that, and I let out a deep exhale. "There is one thing you should know. I was with a call girl just before Scottsdale—"

She stepped back. "Call girl? Have you been tested—?"

"I used protection the whole time, but I didn't know she was a professional. It was all a setup."

Elaine's arms crossed, and her eyes narrowed. "Who set you up?"

All the ground I'd made suddenly felt like quicksand, and I struggled to get us back to that place we'd just been.

My hands went into my back pockets, and I looked down. "Stacy."

"I thought that was over. Is she still in your life, too?"

"No!" I almost shouted. "After I confronted her about it, I don't think I'll ever see her again. I'd better not."

Elaine's arms were still crossed, and she turned to the side, looking down. I waited, watching her.

"Call girls, crazy fiancés, babies everywhere..." The list against me sounded pretty awful, but at the same time, I could swear I heard the faintest glimmer of a change in her tone. "I'm not sure how I feel about this," she said facing me. "Being with someone with so much baggage."

"Technically, none of those things were my fault."

Her eyebrow arched. "You didn't sleep with Kenny?"

"She was on the pill!"

I watched as she chewed her lip, her eyes dropping. "Come here," I said softly, pulling her into my arms. It was a risk, but I was taking it.

"I don't know," she said, but she didn't resist me. She let me hold her.

Her heart beat against my chest, and I lowered my face so that our mouths were a breath apart. I wanted to kiss her so badly. Her chin lifted slightly, and we were right there. But when she spoke, her voice was still a quiet argument.

"I like nice men."

Everything we'd done together flickered across my mind, and I smiled. "No you don't."

With that, I reclaimed those lips. Her arms went around my neck, sending heat flooding to my core. No distance was between us now. We were back, she was back in my arms. Three weeks of wanting her exploded in my chest.

She didn't push me away or tell me no as I kissed her again with more urgency. She turned, and I kissed her cheek.

"I'm too weak when it comes to you," she sighed as I traced the line of her jaw with my lips. "I should be stronger."

My kisses moved to her temple and into her hairline. She was so beautiful, and I had her again. "You're incredibly strong," I murmured. "You held me off for three weeks when everything in me wanted to come here and take you back."

I could feel her breathing pick up as I kissed her, and the tension below my waist grew tighter. My mouth returned to hers, and it opened quickly, tongues uniting, her fingers now threading in my hair. Her lips were so sweet, but I moved my kisses to her chin, dropping down to her neck, and unfastening the buttons on her shirt, kissing every spot of delicate skin that was revealed as it came apart.

"I just ached for you," she said. "At night, all I could remember were your hands. Oh," she gasped as I unfastened her bra and quickly cupped her breasts, sliding my thumbs over her tight nipples.

"What else did you remember?" I leaned down, pulling one into my mouth. She moaned, and I lifted her into my arms, carrying her back to the bedroom. My dick was straining against my pants, and I wanted to taste her, be inside her, have every part of her again. Three weeks was too long to be without her, and my body craved her.

Her hands were on my neck, and her cheek rested on my shoulder. "Every time I saw Cooper, it hurt so much. I thought about everything we'd said, and I wanted it all back."

Spreading her out on the bed, I knelt in front of her, pulling her jeans down, sliding them over her hips along with her thong. "You should've called me," I said as I caught the back of one knee then the other, lifting them and opening her before me.

Her eyes were hooded as I leaned forward to dip my tongue inside. "Oh, god," she moaned. "I couldn't," she gasped, threading her fingers into my hair.

My tongue flattened against the tight little bud nestled between her folds, circling it and teasing it as her hips rocked with my motions. She moaned again, and I almost went off at that delicious sound.

"You can always call me," I said, kissing the crease in her thigh.

She whimpered, and I returned to what I knew she wanted, focusing my attention on the space between her thighs, giving her a little suck and moving my fingers from behind her knees to deep inside her. She moaned and squirmed against my mouth, bucking and quivering as she started to come.

Watching her beautiful body twisting in ecstasy had me aching to be inside her, but I held back. My tongue slid through her folds before returning to the center, where it moved up slowly then flickered back and forth quickly.

"Oh, god!" she cried out, jerking her hips as the orgasm flooded her body. I felt it in her thighs, and I rolled the condom on fast before plunging deep inside to finish together. Her legs wrapped around me as her insides held me tight. All of the pain and longing of the last several weeks vanished in the rush of us coming together like this. Her heart rose up to meet me as our tongues entwined, and through the deep haze of our connection, I felt our souls mesh like two perfectly matched pieces. My puzzle solved.

We rode out the last waves of pleasure until we collapsed against each other, her arms loose around my neck, her cheek on my chest. I felt happy and whole again with her beside me this way. I rolled onto my back, drawing her close against me — my favorite way to hold her. This time I had every intention of keeping her there.

"I love you," I whispered against her ear, kissing her as I watched her cheek rise with a smile.

"I love you," she whispered back.

Relaxing my arms, I allowed her to fall back against the pillow so I could see her lovely face. "I'm sorry I made choices that hurt you."

"You didn't know," she said, trying to roll back to me, but I stopped her.

"Look at me," I said more firmly, and she leaned back again to meet my gaze. "No one will ever mean as much to me as you do. You have my heart. You always will." Tears sparkled in her eyes, and I leaned forward to kiss them away.

"Are you saying you're mine?" she whispered, a tiny smile lifting the corner of her beautiful mouth.

"Yes," I said, kissing that corner. "Will you be mine?"

She rose to meet me and then some, pushing me back against the pillows, opening my mouth with her kiss. I followed her lead, meeting her tongue, my hands moving to the sides of her head, my fingers threading through her silky locks. She pulled her chin up, breaking our kiss and I caught her neck with my mouth. She was on me in a straddle now, and it wouldn't take much for me to be back inside her.

"I'm yours," she gasped before dipping down to cover my mouth briefly. "I've been yours since that first kiss in the desert. Since the day you dropped everything and flew to comfort me when I called. Even these last few weeks, when I wasn't sure how I felt, I was still yours. I'll always be yours. It only hurt because I couldn't bear the thought of anyone else having any part of you."

Rolling her back, I quickly changed my protection, sliding her thighs open and moving back inside her. She only sighed, eyes closed as I rocked our hips in a gentle motion, kissing her neck, her shoulders, nipping her breasts, loving every part of our bodies uniting in this way.

"You have every part of me," I whispered against her skin as I kissed my way back to her mouth.

Our bodies moved faster, friction building until we were both coming again, blinding and gorgeous, her cries of release mixed with mine to form the only sounds we heard. My future, my home, my family—everything was right here in her arms.

Breathing fast, spent, and happy, I dropped down on the bed beside her. She scooted closer to me. "I have one thing to show you."

"What?" I smiled, but she hopped up, heading to the dining room.

I took a moment to straighten the sheets, dispose of the condoms, and prop up the pillows. She was back again holding both our phones and climbed in beside me.

"What is it?" I said, smiling as I watched her nestle down, resting her head on my chest, fitting perfectly under my arm.

"I figured I'd better show this to you so there wouldn't be any misunderstandings later." She touched the face and pulled up a text marked with my name.

"Did you text me tonight?" I asked, tilting the face of her phone so I could see it.

"I had just pressed send when you appeared at my door." She took my phone and put it in my hands. "I knew it was too soon for you to have gotten it."

I switched over to my text messages. "What did you say?"

The light blinked, and I read what she wrote. It was one word.

"Remember how it works?" she said. "If it hurts too much?"

I nodded, realizing now she would never have sent me away. Warmth flooded my entire body as I met her eyes.

*Bubblegum.*

In that one word, I was back. We were both back. Safe and exactly where we belonged.

## Epilogue:
## Elaine

Control. Choosing my own destiny. Firmly holding the reins — these have always been the most important things in my life.

They're why I didn't go to law school, they're probably why I love teaching so much. They're definitely why I stayed with Brian too long. He'd never posed a threat to my independence. He didn't ask me for anything. He made no demands... And we shared the most uninspiring, unromantic, passionless relationship of my life.

Eight months with one man has changed everything.

With a sigh, I lean my head on my hand to watch him sleep. Patrick Knight. I lightly touch his smoky hazel eyes, now closed. My gaze travels up to his light-brown hair tipped with natural gold highlights I beg him not to trim. (They're so beachy!)

My chest rises with the warmth of the overwhelming, out-of-control, completely hopeless love I have for him.

Another first for me — I do *not* fall hopelessly in love. In all of my relationships, I'm the dominant one, the one who calls the shots, decides when it's time to have sex, when it's time to end it. Not with this man.

His lined stomach rises and falls gently with his breathing, and my eyes continue their journey to where the sheet is draped across his waist. A memory of that first night I tied him up flickers through my mind, and heat flares between my legs. God, that had been wild. And incredibly hot. I could still see his muscles rippling as he struggled to get free, and a little shiver runs through me.

That edge between intense love and intense power is absolutely thrilling. He took me so hard... The next day, I'd run away like a scared little girl. I knew in that moment I could never say no to him. He would take everything from me, and I'd give it to him willingly. He was stronger than me, and I loved it. And it terrified me.

Sliding down on the mattress, I press my back into his side and hold up my left hand. A square-cut diamond engagement ring, surrounded by tiny baguettes is on my third finger. A walk on the beach, sunset, I didn't know what he was doing until I felt the cool metal sliding on my finger. Of course I said yes.

"Still like your ring?" his voice is behind my shoulder, low and in my ear, and the sound registers in my core.

"Yes." Turning my face to kiss his nose, his lovely eyes blink slowly, and I smile. "Did you sleep well?"

Strong arms go around my waist, holding me tightly against his chest, like he's afraid I'll slip away.

Like that could ever happen.

"Mm-hm," he breathes, kissing the crook of my neck. Everything inside me lights up at the mixture of love and desire in his voice. I don't have to look down to know what he wants. I can feel it.

"I was just thinking…" A sneaky smile crosses my lips, and I scoot lower in his arms so my ass is pressed into his pelvis.

His hands slide down my stomach and his mouth is right at my ear sending a shiver to my toes. "I like where your head's at."

Every touch has my body tingling. He kisses my shoulder, sending desire blazing through me, and I feel him hard at my back. Dropping my head against his shoulder, I open my thighs.

"My head?" I tease, but it comes out as more of a moan.

"Among other things." His fingers ripple across my clit as he fills me from behind, groaning with each thrust, taking me higher with each push.

I can't help a little cry. He fills me so completely, the pleasure is almost painful. I'm trembling inside, and his fingers massaging my clit have me going blind.

With an exhaled swear, he thrusts deeper, and I can't help arching my back to him. Heat, waves of delicious energy trembling down my legs, deep groans mixed with higher sighs. We've been together all sorts of ways, both of us happy to experiment, but the morning rush, the level of intense desire and urgency gets me every time.

He rolls me onto my stomach, moving faster between my legs, scrubbing my clit against the mattress. My whole body rocks with his thrusts, and the friction has me hotter and more tense… the tightness in my stomach, the growing pressure is so strong, all I know is if he stops, I'll implode.

"Oh, god, more," I beg as he groans, going deeper, harder.

Quivers start in my thighs until at last it tips over the edge. I'm crying out, arching up from the mattress; his head touches my shoulder with a deep groan as he comes. Another pump, and I almost don't want him to stop, another and I'm pushing back against him. One more, and I'm crying out again.

He rocks me a few more times until at last we're gasping and trembling, collapsing into each other's arms amazed and oh, so satisfied. It takes a few moments to come down.

"I love waking up in your bed," he says at last, and I can't help laughing as his strong arms go around me, pulling me to him as we fall back.

"My bed or our bed?"

Patrick started out with his own place in Wilmington. I think his reason was to be sure we weren't rushing into anything. That lasted about a week before he was living in my condo full-time.

"Can I say our bed now?" his brow creases.

"It's been five months, and we're engaged." Bending my elbows, I prop up beside him. "I think you'd better."

He smiles and slides my hair off my shoulder before leaning up quickly to kiss it. "Fine. Our bed."

Pushing completely up, I kiss his lips then head to the bathroom to turn on the shower. "What are you doing today?" I call out, holding my hand under the water.

"Meeting Derek. He's forcing me to wear a suit. A beach wedding, and I have to wear a suit."

That makes me laugh. As handsome as he is, Patrick would wear jeans and polos everywhere if he could get away with it. "Their wedding is going to be gorgeous."

I step into the shower, but I move quickly. Knowing my fiancé, I'll never leave the house if he decides to join me, and while that isn't a terrible prospect, I've got to meet Melissa. I'm out with a towel around me, and as I suspected, he's already at the door wearing his bad boy grin.

"Shit," he says.

I kiss him as I pass. "No time to play, Mr. Knight, I have to meet Melissa to taste cakes."

"What! How did I draw the short straw?" He follows me back to the bedroom, sitting on the bed, watching as I dry off and dig through my underwear drawer. Finally, I throw my towel at his head, but he catches it.

"It's not polite to stare." I pull on a thong and fasten my bra, and I see that little gleam in his eye. Heat simmers low in my stomach. "Stop looking at me that way. I'll be late."

"Melissa won't mind if you're late." The tone in his voice has me moving faster before my resolve wavers.

I drop the filmy sundress over my head and step into my wedge heels. "She will, and she's got Aunt Bea here especially for today."

He exhales dramatically. "So I get to try on suits and you get to eat cake."

"You'll get to sample our top three picks, and Derek has to choose his groom's cake." I lean down and kiss his forehead, skipping back before he catches me. "Tonight."

"Pick one with bubblegum in it," he calls after me.

"You're still not using that word right!" I shake my head as I grab my keys and push out the door. He knows very well how Melissa is about being on time. She's as bad as that Marine she's marrying.

* * *

The stout little lady walks around Melissa's gourmet kitchen as if she's in heaven.

"It's an error in justice that you have a kitchen like this and you don't even cook," she pretend-scolds.

"Aunt Bea" drove in from Baltimore just to spend the day with Melissa, discussing cake options and decoration choices. She's practically Mel's long lost fairy-godmother. The two have been close since before my best friend left Maryland, and Mel's entire pregnancy, she's sent her surprise cupcake care packages.

"Baking never interested me," Mel sighs, leaning against the bar, her pregnant belly a basketball under the tight black dress she's wearing.

Pressing my lips together, I can't help but think of Kenny. She's due to have Patrick's baby any day now, and as much as I want to be okay with it, it still stings. My change in demeanor is not lost on my friend.

Melissa pushes off the bar right into my face. "What's wrong?"

I shake my head and attempt a smile. "Nothing! What are you talking about?"

Instantly, she has my arm in her steel grip. "Be right back, AB. Start without us." And we're out the door, headed down to the ocean.

Taking a deep breath as we approach the pounding surf, I'm again amazed at how karma will just come around and knock your socks off. Melissa spent five years with a lying prick of a husband, who slept with prostitutes and beat her, to living here, steps from the ocean, engaged to Derek Alexander, a.k.a., Mr. Sex on Two Legs, who is devoted to her and treats her like a queen. It's extremely reassuring.

"Now," she says, as we walk quickly down the surf, arms linked as the salty breeze pushes our hair back. "The truth, please. What's wrong?"

Taking a deep breath, I just tell her. "I know it shouldn't matter, but… Oh, god! I still can't stop caring about this whole Kenny thing."

We keep walking, and for a few moments, she doesn't speak. "Lainey," she finally says, "Patrick loves you so much. It's so abundantly clear —"

"I know," I groan, shaking my head. "And I'm sure it says something bad about me that I still don't like it —"

"It says you're a human being. You love Patrick, and she's sharing something deeply personal with him. Something you hope to share with him one day."

"She's having his first son." I can't help it, but my eyes grow warm. "That hurts me so much."

We stop and she pulls me into a hug. "I know." Her voice is quiet, and for a moment we don't move. We just stand there in our strange embrace, me trying to make room for her own growing baby bump.

"Speaking of," I sniff, straightening up and pushing my tears away. "How are you feeling?"

"Five months pregnant." Her voice is more of a groan. "It's the second trimester. I'm supposed to be in the golden days, right?"

My eyes narrow. "Why does that sound like you're not?"

"I think a man must've called it that. So far, I haven't seen any of this pregnancy as being particularly golden."

"And how's Derek doing with it?"

She smiles that secret little smile they share and looks down, cheeks flushing. "He's wonderful."

"Oh my god, you must be the cutest pregnant couple on the planet!" I scoop her arm into mine as we start walking again.

"And you and Patrick are just cute period," she adds. "You know I'm forever one thousand percent on Team Patrick."

"I know," I say as we continue down the shore.

"He made it possible to put Sloan away without me even saying a word." Her tone becomes serious. "I can never thank him enough for that."

I squeeze her hand. "He was so glad he could help you."

"He did. Although I'm sorry that girl... Toni? I hated she had to take a hit."

My lips press together. "No way, she was prepared for it, and she kicked Sloan's ass. He never saw it coming, Patrick said."

"They're my superheroes."

"Patrick and his friendly call girl." I can't help it, I burst out laughing. "Oh my god, Mel, what am I going to do with him?"

"Love him," she declares, laughing. "Keep him."

I shake my head, closing my eyes. "That's the problem. I do love him. I love him too damn much."

"Why is that a problem?"

"It's not," I sigh. "Except he gets away with everything."

Melissa catches her long, brunette spirals in her hand and twists them over her shoulder, turning us back to her home. "That's okay. Patrick's a good boy."

"Oh, no he's not," I snort, my blonde hair flying in the breeze.

"Well, then it's even better," she laughs. "You've never been particularly attracted to good boys anyway."

We're getting closer to her house, and I don't want to lose my chance. I pull her to a stop. "I'm so glad you're with Derek," I say, giving her arm a squeeze. "He loves you so much. All of these good things that have happened for you make me so happy."

"Thanks," she nods, glowing again. "It's all coming back around I think."

"Have you convinced him to move here yet?" On her back porch, we stomp lightly to get the sand off our dry feet.

Derek and Mel have been arguing Princeton versus Wilmington since before they got engaged. Now it's the only thing they don't agree on... when they're not debating baby names.

"I think so," she says, arching a thin, dark brow. "Patrick being here helps me a lot. Another reason he's my boy."

I shake my head, but my phone is buzzing. "Hang on."

Dashing back into the kitchen, I scoop it up.

"It's been doing that since you left." Bea's leaning down, checking the contents of Melissa's double oven.

"Thanks, Bea!" I sweep my finger across the face, continuing into Melissa's living room. "Hello?"

"Elaine, finally!" Patrick's voice sounds slightly panicked, and my pulse ticks higher.

"What's going on?"

"Kenny's in labor. I've got to go to Bayville now," he says. "I hoped you'd come with me?"

My eyes fly around, searching for Melissa. I hear her in the kitchen, and step back into the room. "Kenny's having the baby," I say, covering the phone. "Patrick wants me to go with him—"

"Go!" She cries, shooing me with her hands.

"Can you pick me up here?" I say into the phone.

"Be right there."

\* \* \*

Labor is not what it looks like on television shows. It's fits and starts and awful and scary and ultimately incredible.

We spent the first few hours making small talk. Kenny's labor started a week earlier than predicted, catching her parents in California. They're flying back, and we hope they'll make it in time. Patrick paces around the room, nervous. First he stands behind me, massaging my shoulders too hard, then Kenny grimaces and doubles over in pain, and he's out in the hall trying to find a nurse.

Finally, her contractions become more regular and the labor really starts. I keep trying to leave the room, but with Kenny's mother still somewhere between here and the West Coast, she keeps reaching for my hand. I stand by her shoulder, smoothing back her light brown hair. It's grown much longer through her pregnancy. Her cheeks are rounder, too, and everything about her seems so young and vulnerable. I try to think of anything distracting to say.

"Patrick snores like a lumberjack."

"He does not," she laughs, but quickly gasps, cringing in agony.

"Are you sure you don't want an epidural?" My voice is high, afraid, and she shakes her head fast.

"I don't want him coming into the world all drugged up." Then she screams, and my heart hits the floor.

Nurses are moving rapidly around the lower half of her body, sweeping mattress pads away and holding her legs.

"Oh, shit." Patrick's face is white as a ghost.

"Patrick! Get. Out!" Kenny yells, and he turns on his heel, pushing through the door at once.

Her face is wild, and I wonder if she wants me to go away, too. But then she's back to shaking and crying and breathing fast—and squeezing the crap out of my hand.

"I'm sorry," she says between rapid breaths. "I need to tell him I'm sorry."

"I think he understands." I wince in pain. "He's just like any other guy around this stuff."

"Oh, ow, oh, OH, GOD!!!" she screams again, and I cringe. My hand is going to be permanently disfigured.

"He's crowning," the doctor says. "Almost there…"

Kenny's whole body clenches as her face turns purple. A loud groan-scream snorts through her nose, and I swear every vein on her body pops out. I'm clenching with her, trying to push like that makes any sense, and I can't even feel my hand anymore.

Time, everything, seems to go into slow motion, and in a few moments, her cries are joined by the tiny howls of a baby. Tears flood my eyes as they lift him out, and we're both crying. Kenny's shaking, and everyone is exclaiming how beautiful he is.

"He's here!" Kenny weeps, and I hug her close as they snuggle him to her breast.

"He's here." My voice is hoarse, and tears are all over my face.

I lean my head against hers, and we both gaze down at his little body, reaching and struggling. A halo of golden hair is on his little head, and what appear to be blue eyes wander around both our faces.

"He's so beautiful," Kenny whimpers, and we both lose it again. One of the nurses goes to the door, and Patrick is back with us. He's on the other side of the bed, stretching his arms around Kenny and up to my shoulders, looking down at his little son.

"Check him out." His voice is so warm. I blink back tears, watching him.

"Congratulations," I say, and he leans across the bed to kiss me.

Our eyes hold each other's for a moment, before he winks and leans back down to Kenny. "Look what you did," he says in that funny voice of his.

She reaches up and hugs his neck. "I'm sorry I yelled at you."

He laughs then. "It's okay. I really wanted to get out of here anyway."

"Labor kicks bee sting's ass."

He laughs, but I'm confused. "What?"

Just then the baby lets out a little noise, and we all snap to him. He's reaching and nuzzling against Kenny's breast, and she glances at both of us.

"Smart guy," Patrick teases softly.

"Privacy please," Kenny says, and we both step away—time to eat.

"He's so perfect," I said as Patrick and I cross to the other side of the room.

He signals to the door. "I want to sneak out and get Ken a little something… I don't know what."

"Get her a gold necklace with a little charm that has an emerald on it."

His brow creases. "That's very specific."

"It's the birthstone for May," I say, leaning forward and kissing his cheek. "She'll love it, now hurry."

Strong arms go around my waist, and he scoops me up against him. "Have I told you how much I love you today?"

"Yes," I laugh, kissing him. "And you just had a baby, so hurry back."

He kisses me again harder and then dashes out the door. I only look after him a moment before turning back and crossing over to Kenny's bed. She's nursing the baby and gazing at him with so much love. I completely understand the feeling. He's a glowing little bundle of sunshine.

"He looks just like Patrick," she says, laughing.

I lean over. "With your beautiful blue eyes." Our eyes meet and we smile together, but my heart is heavy. "Is your aunt on the way?"

At once, Kenny's expression changes, and she looks down, pressing her lips together. She almost seems nervous.

"What's wrong?" I glance around before I lean closer. Only one nurse is still in the room, and she doesn't appear to be listening to us.

"Oh, Elaine," Kenny whispers, "I never talked to her."

"I don't understand—"

"Aunt Laura's not coming. I never talked to her about Peanut."

"Peanut?"

"The baby! My dad's going to kill me. Patrick's going to... well, he thinks it's all settled, but I never could do it. I never could get myself to call her."

My heart actually feels a little better at her words. "Are you saying you want to keep him?"

She hesitates, looking down. "I don't know how I could. He's just so beautiful. I just... I couldn't give him up like that."

Her voice breaks, and my heart does as well. We both turn to his sweet little golden head. He's sleeping now, and she hugs him to her breast. I lightly run my finger down his little cheek. With his eyes closed, he looks so contented. All I can think about is watching Patrick sleep this morning.

Tears are in Kenny's blue eyes as she looks up at me again. "I wanted so many times to ask if maybe..." Pausing, she chews her lip. "But I know you hate me—"

"I don't hate you!" I cry. Her eyes narrow, and I blink down. "Okay, this situation has been difficult for me. But it's not a matter of hate. And the baby's just as much Patrick's as he is yours."

"He's so precious." Her voice is full of warmth, and I nod, loving him already.

Trying for encouragement, I give her a nudge. "What did you want to ask so many times?"

Her eyes travel over my face, and I hope she sees my answer waiting there. "I thought about it so much, but I was sure you'd never consider it."

"Consider what?"

"Would you and Patrick... want to keep him?"

My throat constricts, and tears flood my eyes again. Deep inside, I know nothing would be more right. "Is that something you could do?" I can't imagine giving him up now that I've seen him.

She nods slowly. "Little boys need their daddies, and I know Patrick will be good with him. And you're so smart and beautiful—"

252

"I love him already," I say, hoping to put her mind at ease.

Her brow relaxes and she leans toward me. I hug her shoulders, petting the baby again. "And I could still see him sometimes? I mean, if that's okay with you."

"Of course, you'll still see him!" I cry. "You'll see him as much as you want. It's the perfect solution!"

We both start to laugh through our tears, and she hands him to me. His body is tiny, but it's sturdy. I hug him to my chest.

"You look so natural with him," Kenny whispers. "I think... would you talk to Patrick about it? He loves you so much. I know he'll say yes if you're okay with it."

I lean forward and kiss her head. "I'm pretty sure he'd say yes anyway, but I'll talk to him. And you need to call me Lainey."

Relief shines in her eyes. "Thank you, Lainey."

Patrick enters the room, and his face instantly lines with confusion as he takes in the scene. "What'd I miss?" He leans over to check his little son, sleeping against my breast.

I step back and kiss his cheek. "I'll tell you later. Did you get it?"

"This hospital's gift shop is pretty impressive," he says.

"They have a captive market."

With a small flourish, he whips out a white box tied with a blue satin bow and steps to the bed. Kenny's eyebrows rise. "What is it?"

"Open it," Patrick says, grinning and moving behind me, putting his hands on both my shoulders.

We watch as Kenny pulls out the delicate golden necklace with a beautiful, heart-shaped emerald pendant. Tears are back in both our eyes as I hand Peanut to her and then fasten the gift around her neck.

"I love it!" Tears spill down her cheeks.

"Must be all the pregnancy hormones." Patrick rubs the back of his neck.

"You did good," I laugh, wrapping my arms around his waist and leaning my head on his shoulder.

A nurse enters with a clipboard, and Kenny looks up to me. "Would you take him?"

I step forward and lift his little body into my arms again unable to keep from smiling. Patrick comes behind me and puts his arms over mine, resting his chin on my shoulder. I kiss his cheek, noticing his expression has changed. He is *not* smiling.

"What's wrong?" A tinge of worry tightens in my stomach.

He lets out a little sigh. "It's nothing. I guess I just... I didn't think I'd like him so much. Seeing him like this, in your arms. I don't want him to go away."

I couldn't have asked for a better opening. "How would you feel about us keeping him?"

His eyes flash to mine. "What about Aunt Laura—"

"I can explain it more later, but Kenny asked and well... I sort of already said we would."

That gorgeous smile breaks across Patrick's face just before he kisses me, smothering my delighted laugh.

A throat clearing softly then growing louder breaks us up. "Excuse me, guys?" We both turn to see Kenny squinting at us. "I'm all for the love, but I need to ask you about this."

"What is it?" Patrick asks as we approach the bed.

"How would you feel about naming him Patrick Lane Knight?"

Tears and laughter seem to be the order of the day as we all agree. It's perfect.

* * *

By unanimous decision, Lane spends the first several months with Kenny. He's nursing, and she's so in love with him. Even if it's only temporary, and Patrick and I are dying to spoil him rotten, none of us can separate him from his mamma so soon.

Melissa is ecstatic that we're keeping him. "Dex and Lane," she announces over the phone. "Sounds like double trouble."

"I can't wait for you to see him." I'm standing in the spare bedroom of our condo Patrick and I have transformed into a baby haven, complete with stuffed footballs, baseballs, giraffes, and all sorts of baby-boy toys. "He's got bright blue eyes like Kenny, but everything else is pure Patrick."

"I'm sure he's gorgeous."

I kiss her through the phone, ending our call.

"He'll probably end up being an artist," Patrick says, wrapping his arms around my waist as we survey the sports-themed baby room.

Placing my arms over his, I turn to kiss his cheek. "That would be amazing. The only thing that could possibly make you sexier is if you started painting."

He smiles, rotating my body to face him. "Didn't you see all the painting I was doing in here?"

I can't help laughing, but Patrick covers my mouth with his, which leads to an intense make-out session and us back in our bed, rolling around, kissing and making cuddly love, as I call it now. Ever since we've become parents, our love-making had turned into as much touching each other and kissing and wonderment as anything. As if we're suddenly aware what we're doing could result in something as amazing as baby Lane. It's only temporary. I know we'll be back to situations possibly requiring bubblegum before long, but it's very sweet.

Lying contented in Patrick's arms, I run my finger down the line of his chest, kissing his skin and breathing in his warm, soap-laced guy-smell. "Everything's changed," I say, as he kisses the top of my head.

"Mmm." His voice is sleepy. "What's changed?"

I push up on an elbow, and hazel eyes meet mine. "I don't mind anymore. Not at all. In fact, I'm so happy you got Kenny pregnant." A little laugh slips out when I realize what I've just said. "I mean it. Lane is so perfect, and he looks so much like you. I can't believe how much I love him."

Patrick moves a strand of hair off my face, behind my ear. "I love you," he says, and I lean forward to kiss his lips.

"I love you." I feel the need to say it again. "And I love your baby boy."

"*Our* baby boy," he corrects, rolling me onto my back. He kisses my neck, and his words are slightly muffled. "Did you say we were moving up the wedding date?"

I laugh as his kisses rise to behind my ear, his hand moving to my breast. A tingle of electricity flies straight between my legs as his thumb teases my nipple. "We haven't even set a date yet."

His mouth hovers just over mine. "Let's fix that."

Sliding my arms around his neck, I pull our lips together. "You say when, and I'll take care of where." Our mouths open and tongues meet.

256

His lips move to the corner of my mouth. "Tomorrow."

His knee presses between my thighs, and I open them readily, arching my back and smiling. "Let's pick a date we can actually keep."

"Oh, god," he groans as he pushes inside. He's so sexy, I can't help the lovely moan that rises from my throat.

"Tomorrow, please." He bends down to pull a nipple into his mouth.

"Ooh, you're crazy," I gasp, pushing him onto his back and moving into our latest position, his arms wrapped around me, holding me close, my hands over his head, covering his mouth with kisses. My hips rock as pleasure tightens in my core.

We can spend the rest of the night debating dates and making love. It's so much more than I ever dreamed I'd gain when I laid eyes on this man in a restaurant in the desert. Everything we've been through to get here seems worth it now. I have him and our baby and a new friend, and it's all a beautiful treasure — one I'm happy to keep. Always.


~ The End ~

If you enjoyed this book by this author, please consider leaving a review at Amazon, Barnes & Noble, or Goodreads!

Reviews help new readers find your favorite authors, and even help your favorite authors with advertising opportunities.

So please take a moment—even a short, positive review helps!

\* \* \*

Be the first to know about New Releases by Tia Louise! **Sign up for the New Release Mailing list today! (http://eepurl.com/Lcmv1)**

\* \* \*

**Bonus Content:**

\*Read the original, *deleted* Prologue at **http://wp.me/p3C5Uj-2iD**

\*Hear some of the music that inspired *One to Keep* on Spotify! **(https://play.spotify.com/user/authortialouise/playlist/3 j9NoZT0X42W8TcxgfvIDc)**

\*See the images that inspired One to Keep on Pinterest! **(http://www.pinterest.com/AuthorTiaLouise/one-to-keep)**

\* \* \*

**Also by Tia Louise:**

*One to Hold*
(Derek & Melissa's story)

**WARNING: Mature themes, strong language and sexual content. Recommended for adult readers (18+) only!**

Derek Alexander is a retired Marine, ex-cop, and the top investigator in his field. Melissa Jones is a small-town girl trying to escape her troubled past.

When the two intersect in a bar in Arizona, their sexual chemistry is off the charts. But what is revealed during their "one week stand" only complicates matters.

Because she'll do everything in her power to get away from the past, but he'll do everything he can to hold her.

**Standalone, M/F, HEA**

Available on

Amazon | Barnes & Noble | iTunes | Kobo | ARe

Print copies on Amazon | Createspace


**\*\*Coming in 2014:**

-*One to Protect* (a Derek + Melissa novella)
-*One to Love* (Kenny + "Mr. X")

# ACKNOWLEDGMENTS

I have to start by saying a huge THANK YOU!!! to everyone who read, swooned over, and buzzed about my debut adult romance *One to Hold* (Derek & Melissa's story). If it weren't for you guys, I would've abandoned this crazy idea as just a silly flight of fancy. So *Thank you, readers!* I couldn't do this without you.

Specifically, I have to thank my lovely betas and critique partners, who helped me craft *One to Keep* with their eagle eyes, wit, and brilliant detective work—Ginger Sharp (my Princeton pro), Aleatha Romig, Kate Roth, Tami Johnson, Ilona Townsel, KP Simmon, Gretchen de la O, and Heather Carver. You guys are absolutely, without a doubt, the best readers a person could have. Each of you gave me a lightbulb.

I would be nowhere without Mr. TL, who is amazing in every way and gives me brilliant "guy" feedback. I love you, sir.

Huge thanks to my two precious daughters, who never complain when I'm working too long, and who know to not read the computer screen when Mommy's typing...

To my cover designer Regina Wamba, who makes my books absolutely gorgeous. You're the best! And to the publicity queen, KP Simmon—you were my friend first, and I love working with you. Thank you so much for believing in my books.

Finally, to my "Keepers"—Heather, Ilona, Jess, Angela C., Melissa, Jackie, Chrissy, Karrie, Ginger, Jas, Teresa, Louisa, Holly, Daphnie, Amber, Evette, Maria, Rebecca, Lucinda, Jennifer E., Anna, Deanna, Tanya,

Natalie, Ellen, Brandi, Ann, Jennifer L., Jennifer N, Crystal, Nicole, Ali, Richelle, Antoinette, Sara, Angela P., Laura, Chantelle, Molly, Brandelyn, and Katrina—you guys have amazed and touched me with all of your enthusiasm and support. Thank you for keeping me going—I love your guts!

Also a HUGE Thanks to my amazing friends on GoodReads, Lisa P., Claire, Mo, Jen, Rachel, Holly, Linda, Ang, Nichole, and *all* the girls at "Sizzling Pages"—which brings me to all the book bloggers and friends, specifically Liz, Nikki, Sherry, Natasha, Vilma, Angie, Kathy, Autumn, Ali, Lisa and True Story Book Blog, Bridger Bitches, Once Upon a Page, Dirty Hoe's—and far too many more to count...

I love and *appreciate* you all more than I can say.

*Thank you!* <3

# About the Author

Tia Louise is a former journalist, world-traveler, and collector of beautiful men (who inspire <u>all</u> of her stories... *wink*) — turned wife, mommy, and novelist.

She lives in the center of the U.S.A. with her lovely family and one grumpy cat. There, she dreams up stories she hopes are engaging, hot, and sexy, and that cause readers rethink common public locations...

It's possible she has a slight truffle addiction.

**Books by Tia Louise:**

*One to Hold* (Derek & Melissa), 2013
*One to Keep* (Patrick & Elaine), 2014

**Connect with Tia Louise here:**

On Facebook:
https://www.facebook.com/AuthorTiaLouise
On Twitter: @AuthorTLouise
On Pinterest: http://pinterest.com/AuthorTiaLouise
On Instagram: @AuthorTLouise
Email: allnightreads@gmail.com

Made in the USA
San Bernardino, CA
08 July 2014